Everything
I NEVER
Wanted

K. STREET

ISBN-13: 978-1720882381

Dedicated to my girls, Marni and Crystal.
You two are the embodiment of the word tribe.
Thank you for being mine.

PROLOGUE

TUCKER

Shayne laid her head on my shoulder, her baby soft curls brushing against my beard as I rocked us. It was after two in the morning, and I was both physically and mentally exhausted. Unable to keep my eyes open for another second, I dozed off, only to awaken moments later when Shayne stirred.

"Mama?" she whimpered.

Every time she asked for Dani, it gutted me.

"Shh. It's okay, Doodlebug."

I patted her butt and started humming the strains of an Aerosmith song. Her tiny arms went around my neck as she snuggled in closer.

The glow cast from the night-light on the opposite wall illuminated the space enough for me to see the dimple in her cheek. The resemblance to Dani was almost painful. Shayne and I had the same eyes, but she was the miniature version of her mother. From the chestnut brown hair and button nose to the crooked pinkie finger.

How in the hell was I going to do this alone?

I rocked Shayne for a few more minutes before I carefully rose from the chair and walked over to her crib. Just as I started to peel her from my body, she woke up.

"Dada, hold me." Her voice quaked as she tightly clung to me.

"Shh, Bug. It's night-night time."

"Dada, no. Hold me. *Peas.*"

"Okay, baby. Okay." I stood next to the crib and started rubbing small circles on her back, trying to get her to go to sleep.

Once she seemed convinced I wasn't going to lay her down, Shayne rested her head on my shoulder. "Mama at?" she faintly asked into my neck.

I felt her tears on my skin.

The impact of her question struck me with the force of a wrecking ball. I'd tried to explain it a hundred different times and in a hundred different ways. Shayne was barely eighteen months old, so the concept was impossible for her to grasp.

I tried to push the words past the lump in my throat, but I couldn't make myself say them. I was tired of breaking her heart, so instead of answering, I hugged her closer. She wrapped herself tighter around me as we stood clinging to each other like a life raft.

Over the last several months, for one reason or another, sleep had been an elusive mistress. Tonight was no different. I carried Shayne into the living room, grabbed the blanket from the back of the couch, and tossed it onto the recliner.

"Me firsty, Dada."

"Do you want some water?"

"Peas."

I made my way into the kitchen. With Shayne still in my arms, I filled a sippy cup with water and gave it to her. Then, I took her back into the living room. I picked up the remote and settled us into the chair. After I covered us with the blanket, I turned on the television.

"Cars?"

I knew what she wanted, and it wasn't the cartoon.

"Okay, Doodlebug, but you have to close your eyes." I pulled up the shows that I'd saved on the DVR. *Counting Cars* started playing on the screen.

It only took a few minutes before Shayne's eyes grew heavy, and her breathing evened out. Slowly, I reached for the lever on the recliner and raised the footrest, and then I adjusted her in my arms. Shayne's head rested on my chest, tucked into the space where my heart used to be, before my entire world had been turned upside down.

I closed my eyes, desperate to stop the thoughts cycling through my head. I didn't want to think about the circumstances that had led me here.

Back to Jaxson Cove.

Living a life that was everything I never wanted.

1

TUCKER

"Shayne, we're leaving for Grammy's in five minutes," I called out from the front door where I was putting my boots on.

"Be right there, Daddy." Two minutes later, she came into the living room, dragging her backpack behind her. "Ready."

"Did you forget anything?"

"Nope."

"Where's Wilbur?" I asked, referring to the small stuffed pig she took almost everywhere with her.

If she forgot him, things would get ugly come bedtime. That meant I'd more than likely end up driving the thing back out to my mom's later. All Shayne had to do was jut out her bottom lip, and I'd cave like a damn sinkhole.

"He's already in here." She picked up the bag and slid it onto her back.

I reached to open the door for her. "Let's load up."

Shayne ran out of the house, and I locked up behind us and then helped her into the truck.

As I pulled out of the driveway, my eyes darted to the

5

rearview mirror. Shayne sat, staring out the window, with a perplexed look on her face.

"You okay, Bug?" I asked, turning my gaze back in front of me.

"Yep. Just thinking."

"Okay." I decided to wait her out because that was the way it worked with her.

A few minutes later, she spoke, "Daddy?"

"What, Doodlebug?"

"Do you think Mama can see me from heaven?"

Her question seemed to come out of nowhere and felt like a shot straight to my heart. You'd think the ache would've dulled after all this time; if anything, it was worse.

"Of course she can baby."

"Does she have a telescope? Or are there holes in the floor? How does it work? If there are holes, then why can't she fall out and come back to us?"

Each word rained down in a succession of quick blows.

I didn't have all the answers, so I told my daughter the closest thing I had to the truth. "I'm not sure how it works, Bug. I just know it does."

We talked about Dani every day because it was important to keep her memory alive. Shayne had been just over a year old when her mom died. I needed her to know how amazing her mother was. There were things I'd never tell my daughter though. Like how her mother had sacrificed her life for Shayne's.

"Do you think she knows I love her?"

"She knows." I kept my eyes on the road and one hand on the wheel while I reached back with the other. When I felt her small palm slip into mine, I spoke, "I love you, Bug."

"I love you, too, Daddy."

I gave her hand a squeeze and then returned my own back to the wheel.

She was quiet for a minute before she spoke again, "Grammy said she's taking me to get a haircut. Guess what else?"

Relief washed over me as she changed the subject. "What?" My gaze shifted between her and the road.

"She said I can have ice cream before dinner. And I can stay in the bathtub as long as I want. I'm staying in there forever."

"You'll turn into a prune." I caught her wide-eyed look in the mirror.

"I don't want to be a prune. That's what Grammy eats when she's concentrated."

I laughed hard. "You mean, constipated."

"Yes, that." She giggled.

We had another few miles before we made it out to my mom's. She lived on a nice-sized piece of land out in the country, still in the same house where she and my dad had raised me and my brother.

When we pulled up in the driveway, my mother stood on the porch, waiting for us. I barely had the truck in park before Shayne unbuckled the straps of her car seat and reached for the door handle.

"Shayne." My tone was firm as I pinned her with a glare.

She huffed and settled back into her seat.

I was all for her independence, but last weekend, when we had been here for Sunday supper, Shayne had fallen, climbing out of the truck, and skinned her knees. Bug was tough, but she didn't deal well with her own blood, and I didn't want to chance another meltdown.

I exited the truck and moved around to open the door

for her. After I helped her down, she reached into the cab to grab her bag while I leaned over and unlatched her car seat.

Shayne took off like a shot and ran across the yard into her grandma's open arms. As I followed behind her, with the car seat in tow, I took in the landscape and made a mental note to call around for a new lawn service.

"Hi, Mom." I bent to kiss her cheek and set Shayne's car seat on the porch.

"Hi, baby. Thank you," she said and pointed to the seat. "I just put the cover to mine in the wash this morning. I don't know where all those ants came from. I sprayed the car already and vacuumed it, too."

"Want me to buckle it in for you?"

"We'll get it. Won't we, Shayne?" She smiled at her granddaughter, but it didn't quite reach her eyes. "Grammy has warm chocolate chip cookies on the kitchen table."

Shayne squealed as she reached for the screen door handle.

"Doodlebug, put your stuff away before you get a cookie."

"Okay, Daddy."

After she walked inside, my mother intently looked at me. "You doin' okay today, son?"

I nodded. "What about you, Mom?"

"Fine. Just fine."

She'd never been a good liar. Her eyelids were a little puffy, and I could tell she'd been crying. I pulled her into a hug.

Today was Griffin's birthday.

He'd only been eleven months older than me, but that didn't stop him from living up to his role as big brother. Our father died when we were teenagers, and Griffin always looked after us. After he graduated high school, he went into the military. He was killed in action nearly six years ago. My mom had completely fallen apart, and there had been a time I thought I might lose her, too.

"Are you sure you feel up to keeping Bug tonight?" Even though I already knew the answer, today was difficult, and I needed her assurance.

She pulled away to look up at me. "Absolutely. She makes it easier."

I knew exactly what she meant.

"What do you plan on doing with your free night?" She waggled her brows, which made me laugh. The heaviness from seconds ago dissipated.

"You're relentless. We're not having this conversation again."

Laura Jaxson was a stubborn woman, and I wasn't the least bit surprised when she continued on as though she hadn't heard me. "Maybe you should try one of those dating sites."

"There's only room in my life for two ladies. You and Bug." I crossed my arms and looked down at her.

Before Dani, there had been Holly, and there was no way in hell we were going there. After Dani, it wasn't about me, and there wasn't room for anyone else.

"Tucker, you can't hit it and quit it for the rest of your life."

I nearly choked. "You realize you just insinuated that your baby boy is a man-whore, right?"

If she only knew how far that was from the truth. While I did have the occasional no-strings hook-up, most of the time, the only action my dick got came by way of my own hand.

"Tomato, tomahto. It's been a long time, Tuck. Don't you want to love again ... to let yourself be loved?"

"Mom." My tone held a warning.

"Tucker, baby, you've got to start living."

"You make it sound so easy. But it isn't just me. Bug and I are a package deal, and that makes it a million times more complicated. I'm so busy living and taking care of her; there isn't much time left for anything else."

Shayne was my priority, and the last thing she needed was to become attached to someone who might decide the role of stepmom wasn't part of her life plan.

"Honey, I just worry about you two; that's all."

"Stop worrying. I hear it makes you age faster," I teased in an attempt to lighten my darkening mood.

"Tucker Jaxson, don't you make fun of your mother." She placed her hands on her hips and glared up at me.

"Mom, I'm fine. We are fine." I pulled her in for one more hug. "I promise." I released her and called out to my daughter, "Shayne, I'm leaving."

She barreled out of the house, a cookie in each hand. Chocolate was smeared across her cheek. "Gof you one," she said, her mouth full.

"Thank you." I took the cookie and then bent down to hug her. "Be a good girl for Grammy. I'll see you tomorrow. And quit stuffin' your mouth so full."

"'Kay. Love you, Daddy." Shayne squeezed my neck tight.

I planted a kiss on her head. "Love you, too, Bug." I ruffled her hair and kissed my mom on the cheek. Then, I made my way back to the truck.

Shayne was my whole world, but damn, I needed some downtime.

With my fishing pole in the truck bed and a six-pack in the cooler, I drove a few miles, then pulled onto the highway, and went toward the creek. On the way, I spotted an older model Honda parked on the shoulder. The open hood made it obvious the driver was having some sort of car trouble. I slowed down and eased in behind it.

I approached the driver's door and opened my mouth to speak but stopped short. The woman inside had just let loose a string of curse words that left me slightly amused and impressed. She was having a full-blown tantrum that could've rivaled Shayne's.

I let out a low whistle.

Her eyes went wide as she took me in. Blue irises stood out against her black hair. Her hand went to her chest, pressing against her heart. The movement drew my eyes down to the swell of her breasts. She was frightened, but damn, she was beautiful.

2

CAMRYN

I loaded the last of the boxes into my car and slid behind the wheel, ready to put the last several months behind me. I put my key in the ignition, and relief flowed through me when the engine finally kicked over. My car, Lucille, badly needed a tune-up. It was on my to-do list—along with about a million other things.

Years ago, Dad had bought Lucille for me for my fifteenth birthday. We'd spent countless hours together, bent over the hood as he rebuilt the engine. He'd taught me how to swap out a tire, check all the fluids, and change the oil. I loved this car because it was a piece of him. Of our bond. It was one of the only tangible things I had left.

On a heavy sigh, I backed out of the drive and turned the wheel in the direction of the highway. After a few miles, I merged onto I-75 and headed south. The drive from Booker Ridge, Georgia, to Jaxson Cove, Florida, would take me around two hours. My former life faded further away with every mile I drove.

Good riddance.

There wasn't a thing left in Booker Ridge that I'd miss ...

except for my dad. But talking to a marble grave marker wasn't the same as talking to him.

It'd always been me and him against the world until six months ago. He'd had a massive heart attack while mowing the lawn. Here one minute and gone the next. The loss of my father had set a domino effect in place, and now, the remnants of my life closely resembled the aftermath of a natural disaster. It was impossible to rebuild on top of everything I'd lost in Booker Ridge.

I needed to put distance between me and the past, and I was well on my way to a fresh start. I'd landed a new job as the school nurse at Jaxson Cove Elementary and leased a house. I longed for a place where the wounds inflicted on my heart would begin to heal. Somewhere I wouldn't stand a chance of running into my former fiancé around every corner because that shit got old fast.

Fucking Jared.

Jared was the son of a bitch who had made me into the worst kind of cliché. He didn't deserve to occupy space in my head or my heart.

I followed the signs for the I-10 interchange and forced my thoughts to shift to the new job I'd be starting soon. I thought about my new place and the furniture scheduled for delivery this afternoon. I wondered what it would be like to live within ten miles of the Atlantic Ocean and spend my weekends at the beach. For the first time in months, it felt like there was a tiny beam of light at the end of the tunnel.

A few miles outside of town, that feeling flew straight out of my open window. My engine light came on, and then the car started to stall.

"This is not happening."

My fingers tightly gripped the steering wheel as I coasted onto the shoulder. When the car came to a complete stop, I reached for the key to shut off the ignition. Then, I balled my fists and beat them against the steering wheel.

This was the last thing I needed right now.

"Are you kidding me?" I yelled to no one and pulled the hood release.

I opened my door, got out of the car, and then glided my hand over the metal. Carefully, I lifted the hood and studied the engine compartment. There wasn't any sign of smoke, and I had plenty of gas, which meant, more than likely, it was the battery.

Knowing AAA was my only hope, I got back in the car, closed the door, and searched my purse for my cell. After I unearthed it from the bottomless pit, I tried to unlock the blackened screen, but it was pointless. My phone was dead. Typically not a big deal—unless the car battery was dead, too. In that case, you were screwed six ways to Sunday.

"Son of a bitch." I smacked the steering wheel again. "Fuckity, fuck, fuck!" I yelled. "Damn it, Lucille! This is bull-shit." There was something about screaming at inanimate objects that always made me feel better.

A low whistle caught my attention. The source of the noise stood just outside my car door. I pressed a hand to my rapidly beating heart as my eyes shifted upward. Tall, broad, and easily the sexiest man I'd ever laid eyes on stood there, casting a shadow over my face. He was huge but not in an ominous way.

"You damn near gave me a heart attack." I tried to calm down. It took all of point-two seconds for it to dawn on me that he'd probably witnessed my entire meltdown. Morti-fied, I covered my face. "Oh God," I said into my palms. With my hands still hiding my face, I spread my fingers apart and peeked through the cracks. Now would be the perfect time for a crater to open in the ground and swallow me. "Did you see all of that?"

A low chuckle rumbled from deep in his throat. "I heard it, too, and I must say, it was pretty damn impressive." He smiled the sexiest smile I'd ever seen. "I didn't realize *fuckity* was a word."

I dropped my hands from my face and imparted some useless knowledge. "I didn't even make it up. It's in the Urban Dictionary."

"Is that right?"

"It's true. Urban Dictionary is a gold mine."

"I'll keep that in mind. You look like you could use some help."

"It was the open hood, wasn't it? Totally gave myself away." I grinned.

"I know a thing or two about cars. I'll be happy to have a look."

He was attractive and charismatic ... but then again, so was Ted Bundy. Slowly, I slipped my hand into the passenger seat, reaching for the Taser my dad had given me last Christmas. At the time, I'd thought he was just being overprotective; now, I was thankful for his foresight. I'd seen *America's Most Wanted*. Statistically speaking, the sexy stranger standing outside my window probably wasn't going to murder me, but I wanted him to know I wasn't going to go down without a fight.

I held the Taser up and pinned him with a menacing glare, which made me look about as threatening as a litter of puppies. "You seem like a really nice guy, but just in case you get any ideas, I want you to know that I'm not afraid to use this thing."

He held his hands up in surrender. "Relax. I'm not going to hurt you."

"Did you read that in the serial killer handbook?" I joked.

He laughed. Hard. And I found myself relieved because I was pretty sure serial killers didn't laugh like that.

"I'm just here to help, I promise."

I skeptically eyed him. It was balls hot, my phone didn't even have enough juice to power it up, and I had no way to charge it. My options were limited at best.

"Thanks. I appreciate it."

"So, what happened? Did you run out of gas?"

"No, I still have a quarter of a tank. I think it's the battery."

He folded his arms over his chest, which only served to draw more attention to his biceps and the thick veins that ran up his forearms. My tongue trailed across my bottom lip because ... damn, those arms. A backward ball cap sat on his head. My eyes focused on the bead of sweat that had formed below the rim of the cap. His neatly trimmed beard had me imagining all kinds of things. The black sunglasses he wore hid his eyes, and I found myself wondering what color they were.

"Mind if I have a look?"

"Not at all."

He walked to the front of my car to inspect the engine.

Since I was basically a sitting duck, there wouldn't be any harm if I got out, so I did. If the sexy Samaritan tried anything, I'd tase his ass before I ran like hell. I walked around the rear of the car on the passenger's side and made my way up to the front, stopping a few feet from him.

His gaze shifted from the battery to my face. "Are you new in town or just passing through?"

"New."

"Well, welcome to Jaxson Cove." After another minute, he said, "Go ahead and try to start it."

I walked over to the driver's side, leaned in through the window, and dropped the Taser on the seat. I figured, if he hadn't tried to kidnap me yet, he probably wasn't going to. When I turned the key, nothing happened.

"Hang tight. I have jumper cables in my truck."

I watched him as he strolled away, allowing myself a minute to appreciate the way his black T-shirt clung to him and how his jeans fit that ass just right. There was no denying the man was sexy as hell.

The road wasn't busy, so it didn't take more than a few minutes for him to do a U-turn, open his hood, and attach the cables. "Try it now."

This time, when I turned the key, I breathed a sigh of relief. Lucille started right up. My face broke into a wide smile as I returned to the front of the car.

He took off his sunglasses and hung them on his shirt, revealing the most gorgeous set of hazel eyes I'd ever seen. I couldn't tell if they were brown with green flecks or green with brown flecks. I felt the heat of his gaze as those eyes traveled over me.

"Thank you …" I awkwardly stuck out my hand, realizing we hadn't exchanged names.

"Tucker," he replied, sliding his palm into mine. "And you're welcome."

The skin-to-skin contact sent an unexpected tingle up my spine. I couldn't explain it. All my nerve endings seemed to have a heightened sense of awareness brought on by his touch. He expectantly looked at me, and I knew I was supposed to say something, but I couldn't remember what.

"You are?" His eyes never left my face as he shook my hand.

"Camryn."

"Well, Camryn, drive safe." He released me and offered a smile that showed off a row of perfect white teeth.

"Let me pay—"

The look he gave me cut off my words. "Don't finish that sentence."

I wanted to argue with him but refrained. "Thanks again, Tucker."

"You're welcome again."

I got behind the wheel and waited as he removed the cables and then shut the hood. Tucker tapped the metal twice with his open palm, signaling that I was all set. After I plugged my phone into the charger, I watched him for a minute before I pulled back onto the highway and drove toward town.

I slowed my speed when I approached Main Street. Brick buildings housed quaint shops, and the gas-light lampposts that dotted the sidewalks created a picturesque backdrop. It felt safe. Like the sort of place where people left their doors unlocked, neighbors looked out for each other, and everyone knew everyone else's business.

I parked along the curb in front of Jaxson Realty, rolled up the windows, and got out of my car. Since I just needed to run inside to grab the keys to my place, I left Lucille running. I didn't want to chance the battery dying for a second time, and I had to meet the delivery truck in less than thirty minutes.

A bell chimed as I opened the door and went inside.

An older woman sat behind a large desk. "May I help you?"

"Yes, I'm looking for Macy Caldwell."

"You wouldn't by chance be Camryn Parker, would you?"

Her smile was warm and friendly, and the nameplate on her desk read *Doris*.

"That's me," I said, returning her smile.

"Just one second, dear." She picked up the phone and pressed a button. "Camryn Parker is here."

Macy and I had gotten to know each other a bit over the last several weeks through emails and phone calls.

My circle was small, though nonexistent was more accurate. Dad and I had moved a lot when I was younger. We'd never stayed in one place for more than two or three years, which made friendships difficult. At my previous job, most of my former coworkers had been younger than me. Don't get me wrong; twenty-six wasn't old either, but they had practically been babies who loved gossip and drama. Grayson, my best friend from college, had spent the last two years backpacking through Europe. Our last email correspondence was three weeks ago when I'd updated him with my contact information.

So, while I hadn't been awesome at the friend thing in the past, I hoped to change that.

Minutes later, Macy emerged from down the hall. A striking redhead, she looked to be around my age. Dressed in an emerald-green top, fitted black skirt, and heels, she approached me and stuck out her hand. "Camryn, it's so great to finally meet you. Welcome to Jaxson Cove."

People seemed a hell of a lot nicer here than they did in Booker Ridge. Those who disputed whether or not Florida was part of the real South must've never set foot in this town.

Macy's smile was wide, and after we shook hands, she gave me a manila envelope. "Inside you'll find your keys, a copy of the lease, and even some takeout menus."

"Thank you so much. You didn't have to go to all this trouble."

"Nonsense," Macy said. "It's no trouble at all. You have my number. Once you get settled, call me, and we'll go out for coffee or something."

"I'd like that," I said truthfully.

"Wonderful. Is there anything else you need?"

"Nope. I think this is it. Thanks again. It was nice to officially meet you." I smiled at Macy and then turned my attention to Doris. "It was nice to meet you, too, Doris."

"Likewise, dear."

"Have a good day, ladies," I called over my shoulder.

Then, I got back in my car, hit up a drive-through, and drove toward my new home, praying the entire way that I wouldn't be late.

A huge grin spread over my face when I pulled up to the house. It was charming, slate gray with white trim and a red front door that gave it a pop of color. Until now, I'd only seen pictures and taken the virtual tour on the realty website.

Anxious to see the interior, I grabbed the keys from the envelope and made my way inside. The home was older but recently remodeled to include stainless steel appliances, granite countertops, and hardwood floors. An entryway led into a living room; beyond that was the kitchen. A small island anchored the space, and an alcove off the kitchen housed a washer and dryer. A sliding glass door led to a screened-in back porch. It was only a two bedroom, but the master was huge even if it did have only a half-bath with a small shower. The full bath was located down the hall.

It was perfect, and for at least the next year, it was mine.

3

TUCKER

I hadn't been able to get the raven-haired beauty from earlier out of my head. If I were lucky, maybe I'd stumble upon her at the local watering hole, which was how I ended up at The Hideaway. In search of her, I walked in and took a seat at the bar, hoping that maybe running into Camryn was in the realm of possibilities. I ordered a beer, and while I waited, I glanced around the room.

No fucking way.

Instead of Camryn, my eyes landed on the last person I'd ever expected to see. At the other end of the bar sat the woman who had fucking destroyed me. I watched as she finished the last of her beer, set the bottle on the bar, and moved in my direction. She looked better than I remembered. Her low-cut shirt showed off her perfect tits. However, I'd have to be drunk and then some to go there again. Wordlessly, she sat on the empty stool beside me.

Mack set my beer on the bar. "Need anything else, Tucker?"

"Thanks, Mack. I'm good."

He turned to the woman at my side. "What about you, Holly?"

That was the thing about Jaxson Cove. It was a small town, and it didn't matter how long you had been gone. Nobody forgot who you were, what you'd done, who you'd done it with, or who you'd done it to.

"I'll have another Blue Moon."

"Comin' right up."

"Holly Jacobs," I said, without looking at her.

"Tucker Jaxson." Her tone was sugary sweet.

"What the hell are you doing here?" I took a long pull from my bottle.

"Came home to visit my mama. Didn't expect to run into you, but I'm glad I did."

Just then, Mack placed Holly's beer on the bar.

"Thanks, Mack," she said.

He nodded and walked away.

"Your mama ... she okay?"

Mrs. Jacobs was a good woman. I couldn't hold her daughter against her.

"Mama's fine." She traced her finger over the top of her bottle.

"That's good." I needed to get the fuck out of this bar. Dredging up the past wouldn't do a damn bit of good. "Take care, Holly."

"Tucker, wait. Where are you going?"

"Home." I reached into my wallet, threw a twenty on the bar, and headed for the door.

After all this time, I'd thought I'd be numb, but that wasn't the case. I felt the anger take hold, and I needed to walk away. Just as the door closed behind me, it flung open again.

"Tucker! Can you just talk to me?"

"There's nothing to talk about," I called over my shoulder.

"We had plans."

"That was a long time ago," I reminded her and kept walking.

"I loved you." She tried again.

"Not enough."

"Don't you think I deserve to be forgiven after all this time?" She pushed.

That stopped me in my tracks. I turned and strode back to her. "What did you just say?"

"I want you to forgive me." She took a step toward me.

Holly had some fucking nerve.

"For which part? You walked away."

"Tucker, I couldn't stay."

My fists clenched at my sides. "Yes, you could have. You didn't want to stay. You had a choice, and you chose wrong."

"No, I didn't. You did." She pointed an angry finger in my face. "You were supposed to pick me."

I stepped into her personal space. Close enough that I nearly choked on her too-sweet perfume. My voice dropped low, and I spoke through clenched teeth, "That right there is the reason I never did. You only ever cared about yourself. You want my forgiveness? You've got it. You stopped mattering to me a long fucking time ago."

"Tucker, please," she begged and then swiped at her face. "How can you say that? We were everything to one another."

"That was a lifetime ago. There's no going back. Knowing what I know now, there's not a chance in hell I would."

Her sobs drowned out all other sounds. I made no move

to comfort her as she cried. Her tears didn't work on me. Not anymore.

I didn't want to hear another word she had to say.

"Good-bye, Holly." I got in my truck and drove away.

When I arrived home, I headed straight to the kitchen, opened the small pantry, and reached for the bottle of scotch I kept hidden in the back. Then, I grabbed a glass, poured two fingers of whiskey, and carried both into the living room, placing the bottle on the end table. With the glass still clenched in my hand, I sat down on the couch and brought the alcohol to my lips.

I wanted to quiet the chaos. Dull the memories that flashed before me.

When I'd gotten the phone call about my brother, Griffin, Holly and I had come back to Jaxson Cove. Everything around me was falling apart, and I was doing my damnedest to put it back together. I stayed ... but Holly left. Staying had been the right decision. I had known it then, and I sure as hell knew it now.

I emptied another two fingers of scotch into my glass after I finished the first. Then, I got up from the couch, returned the bottle to the pantry, and carried the glass into my room where I finished it off before I got into the shower to scrub off one of the worst days I'd had in a long time.

The following morning, I woke up with a headache. I chugged two bottles of water and popped some ibuprofen. I knew it had more to do with Holly than the scotch. If I never saw her again, it'd be too fucking soon. Needing to get my mind off last night, I walked outside, intending to get the paper, but stopped when I saw a familiar-looking

Honda parked in the driveway next door with the hood up.

The same sexy spitfire from yesterday was bent over, peering into the engine compartment. My eyes moved upward from her toned legs to over her perfect ass covered in a pair of white shorts. I needed to have a closer look. The paper was forgotten as I strode in her direction.

She raised an arm to shield her eyes from the sun. "Tucker. Hi."

"Hello, Camryn."

Her long, dark hair was in a ponytail, and a pink tank top covered her perfect chest. *Damn, she was hot.*

"Tucker"—surprise was evident in her voice—"this feels sort of like fate or kismet or whatever," she said.

Maybe it was.

"Sure ... if you believe in that sort of thing," I replied. "Is it the battery again?"

She nodded. "Pretty sure. I should've gotten one yesterday, but I was having furniture delivered, and I had to be here to meet the truck."

I had two options. Either I could jump her battery again or I could seize the opportunity to get to know her. It didn't have to mean anything.

"Give me ten minutes, and I'll give you a lift into town to pick up a battery. I have a few errands to run anyway."

"You don't have to do that."

"I think I do. I'm certain there's some sort of neighbor code."

"A code?" She grinned, seemingly amused.

"Yeah. Like, if your car battery needs to be replaced, I should give you a lift. If you go out of town, I'm supposed to water your plants, but honestly, your plants would probably die."

She fought against a smile but lost, her full pink lips turned up at the corners. She was stunning.

"What do you say?" I asked, forcing my eyes from her mouth.

She looked thoughtful, and I knew her answer before she spoke the words, "I'd like that. Thank you."

"I'll see you in ten minutes."

She nodded, and then we went in opposite directions.

After a quick shave and a cup of coffee, I opened my front door and found Camryn with her ass leaning against my truck.

"Ready, neighbor?" she asked.

"I am." I opened the passenger door for her.

"And they claim Southern hospitality is dead." She placed her purse on the seat and stretched for the *oh shit* handle.

Damn. That ass.

Camryn reached for her seat belt, and when she turned to buckle it, I shut the door and walked around to my side. Once inside, I started the truck and backed out of the driveway. Camryn leaned hard against the door panel and sat with her body angled in my direction. I pushed the power lock button, and the mechanical sound echoed through the cab.

She raised her brows in question. "I thought we agreed you weren't a serial killer."

"I'm not. You're just leaning into that door pretty damn hard, and I don't want you to fall out."

"So, you're concerned for my safety? That's good."

"Why is that good?"

"It means, chances are, you're not a psycho, waiting for the right moment to dismember my body and hide the pieces in the woods." She gave me a wry smile.

I found her sarcastic wit sexy as hell. "You're safe," I assured her. "So, Camryn, what brings you to Jaxson Cove?"

She glanced out the window before she looked back at me. "It was time for a change, and after landing a new job, I jumped at the chance."

My own story wasn't something I wanted to disclose, and tit for tat wasn't my style, but still, the job had me curious. "Really?"

"Yep. I'm the new nurse for the elementary school."

That meant she'd see plenty of Shayne and not only because we lived next door. If I mentioned I had a daughter, it would be inviting an inquisition. *How old is she? Are you married?* The truth would result in pity, and I didn't need it or want it, so the topic was off-limits.

"Guess that means Mrs. Henderson finally retired. About damn time. She was ancient when I was a kid."

"Wow. You grew up here?"

"Born and raised."

"You never wanted to leave?"

Nothing was further from the truth, but if I answered honestly, she'd ask more questions I'd rather avoid.

"What can I say? This town has quite the hold on me."

I couldn't wait to get the hell outta here, and for a while, I had. When Griffin had died, everything had changed. Regardless that I never intended to come back and build a life here, that was exactly what had happened. Staying away had never been an option.

4

CAMRYN

This morning, after Tucker had taken me to the auto parts store, we had come back to my house, and he'd replaced my car battery. I knew how, but he was neighborly and chivalrous, and for once in my life, I wasn't going to argue if a man wanted to do something nice for me. Afterward, when I'd offered to pay him, he'd shot me down again. This time, I had argued, but he wouldn't budge.

Then, I'd remembered something my Nonna, my dad's mom, had always told me.

"The way to a man's heart is through his stomach."

It gave me an idea. Not that I was after Tucker's heart. Tucker's body though, that might be a different story.

I really needed to stop lusting after my neighbor, so I focused my attention on unpacking some of the boxes. When I finished with that, I went to the grocery store. While I was there, I picked up the ingredients to make brownies. As soon as I got home, I made a batch and put them in the oven.

Tucker had come to my rescue twice in as many days, and I was pretty sure he wouldn't turn down chocolate.

Besides, other than Macy, I didn't really know anyone here, and it would be nice to have a friend.

I pulled the decadent goodness from the oven, turned it off, and then walked down the hall to the bathroom. I gave my reflection a once-over. My wavy jet-black hair sat in a messy bun high on the top of my head, cocoa powder dusted my right cheek, and a glob of raw brownie batter had landed on my tank top in the center of my left boob, bestowing me with a chocolate nipple.

"Oh my God." I laughed out loud.

I washed my face, changed my shirt, and unraveled my hair from its nested perch before brushing my fingers through it.

I went back to the kitchen and carefully cut the semi-cooled-down brownies into something that resembled squares and placed them on a plate. After I slid on a pair of flip-flops, I grabbed the dish and made my way over to Tucker's.

I knocked on the door and waited for an answer. It took long enough that I almost went home. When the door finally swung open, I wondered if it was some sort of parlor trick. Then, I heard a small voice and lowered my gaze.

"Good evening. May I help you?" A little girl stood in the doorway. Her long, dark hair was still damp. She wore pajamas with race cars on them, and there was a small dimple in her cheek. She was beautiful.

"Um ... hi. I'm Camryn."

"Are you here to see my daddy?" she asked politely.

Daddy?

"Yes, I am."

"Daddy, Camryn is here." She planted her hands on her hips and waited.

Just then, Tucker appeared from behind her. "Bug, you

know you aren't allowed to answer the door. We've been over this."

She looked up at him and smiled the most adorable toothy grin that I knew had gotten her out of trouble a time or two. "I forgot."

Tucker scooped up the little girl. "It's all right. Just don't let it happen again." Then, he turned his eyes on me. "Camryn ... hi. What are you doing here?" Surprise filled his words.

"Since you wouldn't let me pay you, I thought a neighborly gesture was in order."

I offered the plate to him, and he stared at it for a long moment before accepting it.

"Shayne, say hello to Camryn. She moved in next door."

She expectantly stuck her hand out. "Pleased to make your acquaintance."

I laughed while stretching out my hand to shake hers. "Hi, sweet girl." I smiled at her.

"You made those for us?" Her eyes widened, and she licked her lips.

"I sure did."

She looked at her father. "Um, Daddy, those look super yummy." Shayne scrunched her brows and pursed her lips. "Aren't you going to see if she wants to come in?"

Tucker remained silent. Suddenly, everything felt awkward, and I knew coming here had been a mistake.

"You know what? You two go ahead and enjoy them." I turned on my heels to go.

"Camryn, it's fine. You can come in." He might have said the words, but it seemed like the last thing he wanted.

I almost declined again, but when I looked at his little girl, her eyes full of hope and curiosity, I knew my answer. She was cute, and I wanted the company.

"Please," Shayne said in her endearing, small voice. "Nobody ever comes over, except Grammy. Oh, and Uncle Nash and Aunt Macy, but they never bring brownies."

When she said Macy's name, I wondered if her aunt and my real estate agent were one in the same, but I didn't think now was a good time to ask.

My eyes found Tucker's. "Are you sure?"

"He is," Shayne answered for him.

"I am." He tilted his head, signaling I should follow.

I should've probably just gone home, but then Shayne had said please, and I knew there was no way I could tell her no.

In his truck earlier, there hadn't been anything to give the indication that Tucker had a child, but inside the house, her presence was everywhere. A small stuffed pig sat on the coffee table next to a coloring book and crayons. One of those huge, plastic race tracks had been set up in the corner, and beside it was an array of small cars arranged by color and size. Framed snapshots sat on the shelves of the wooden entertainment center, and situated in the middle was a big screen television. Positioned adjacent to the couch was a well-worn recliner.

The scene reminded me of my own childhood, ramming me with a pang square in the chest. For a split second, I missed my dad so much, I found it hard to breathe, but I managed to push the emotion down and continued into the kitchen.

Tucker set the brownies on the table and put Shayne down. He grabbed two glasses and a cup for Shayne from a cabinet and then opened the fridge. That was when I saw the picture. Kept in place by a magnet was a photo of a woman and her family. She was thin, and I knew, if I stepped closer, I would see dark circles under her eyes. An

IV pole stood near the head of the bed. She sat on the side of the mattress, legs dangling off the edge. On her lap, she held a much younger version of Shayne, and Tucker wrapped his arms around them from behind.

"You can sit here."

I felt a tug on my hand, but I couldn't force my eyes from the picture until the door closed.

Tucker's eyes briefly caught mine, and I knew he was aware of what I'd been looking at.

"Are you coming?" She tugged again.

I focused on Shayne. "Right here?" I pointed to a chair.

"Yep."

Tucker placed the milk on the table, sat down, and then lifted his daughter onto his lap.

Shayne took a bite of her brownie. "These are yummi-licious."

"I'm glad you like them." I took my first bite and moaned. "So good."

Tucker's gaze fixed on my mouth.

I felt Shayne watching me.

"You're pretty," she said.

"So are you," I told her.

"Daddy says I look just like my mama."

Tucker sucked in a breath, and a pained look flashed across his face. I averted my gaze to take in his kitchen, not wanting him to feel as though he were under a microscope. It was on the smaller side, nothing fancy by any stretch. Instead of stainless steel and granite, it was gray Formica and black enamel. Simple and basic but homey.

"Eat up, Doodlebug. It's almost bedtime." The sound of Tucker's voice drew my attention back to the table.

Shayne stuffed her small brownie into her mouth, oblivious to her father's earlier reaction when she'd mentioned her mother. "You're a good baker." Only it came out more like *baffer* because her mouth was full.

"Thanks," I said.

The room fell silent as we finished up.

"Doodlebug, tell Camryn good night and go brush your teeth. I'll be there in a minute."

"Daddy," she whined.

"Bug." His tone was firm.

"Fine," she grumbled and slid off his lap. She stood in front of me and smiled sweetly. "Lovely to meet you. Next time, can you bring cupcakes with sprinkles? Oh, and pink frosting."

I stifled a laugh. "I'll see what I can do."

"Night, Camryn."

"Good night, Shayne," I said.

Shayne turned back to Tucker, kissed his cheek, and said, "Daddy, don't forget, you promised two chapters tonight."

"I didn't forget. Go on. I'll be right there."

I watched as she skipped into the living room and snatched the little pig off the table. Then, she disappeared around the corner.

"Thank you." Tucker stood, making it obvious it was my cue to leave.

I rose to my feet and pushed in the chair. "It's the least I could do." I folded my arms over my chest and lowered my gaze before I looked up to meet Tucker's eyes. "Why didn't you tell me about her?"

"Why would I?"

"I don't know. We made small talk. I guess I thought you would've mentioned a kid during our conversation in the truck."

"Well ... I'm not in the habit of telling strangers my life story."

"Technically, we're neighbors," I teased, trying to lighten the mood.

Gone was the carefree man from earlier today.

"Being neighbors doesn't make us friends." There was an edge to his tone, which made the words feel harsh.

Something had changed, and I knew it had to do with me being in his space.

"I'm sorry ... I mean ... I just thought ..." I didn't even know what I thought.

He was right; he didn't owe me any details about his life.

"Okay. So ... I'm going to go. Good night, Tucker." Purposeful strides carried me through his house. My fingers gripped the doorknob, and I gave it a twist.

"Good night, Camryn," he called to my back.

I walked out, closing the door behind me.

5

TUCKER

I remained in the kitchen and stared at the back of the door Camryn just walked out of. She'd been occupying my thoughts more than I'd like to admit. Nothing could've prepared me for the sight of her earlier as she stood on my porch, bearing baked goods like some sexy-as-sin modern-day Betty Crocker.

As I thought of her again, an internal battle waged within me. Unless you counted my mom and Macy, I'd never asked a woman into my home. Never taken a woman in my bed. Even on the occasions when Shayne stayed with her grammy.

This had been our home. Mine and Shayne's and Dani's. Not once had a woman I felt an attraction to been granted access through that doorway.

Until tonight.

I glanced to the chair where Camryn had previously sat and then at the glass she'd used that was still on the table. The one her perfect pink lips had wrapped around. I picked it up and traced my thumb over the rim where her mouth had been. I'd wanted to savor her. To sample the chocolate from her lips. The way she'd moaned when she bit into her dessert made me think about all the sounds I'd like to elicit from her.

When Shayne had made the comment about how she looked so much like her mom, it was like being backhanded. I had been sitting across from Camryn, fantasizing about all the ways I wanted to taste her, at the same fucking table I'd once shared with my deceased wife. Rationally, I knew it didn't make sense. Dani was gone. Still, that didn't stop the bitter taste of betrayal from coating my tongue.

The look on Camryn's face. How she'd stammered an apology. I'd needed her gone because it was easier to push her away than deal with my conflicted emotions. Still, I felt like an asshole. Regardless, it didn't change anything.

"Daddy, I'm waiting." Shayne's voice carried through the house and brought me back to reality.

"I'm coming, Bug." I got up from the table and carried the dishes to the dishwasher. I shifted my focus to my daughter as I walked down the hall to her bedroom.

Shayne leaned against her pillows. "Come on, Daddy," she urged, patting the spot beside her.

I pulled back the quilt, the one Mom had made from Dani's old concert T-shirts, and slid in next to my baby girl. She passed me the yellowed and worn copy of *Charlotte's Web*, the one that had belonged to Dani when she was just a girl and curled into my side. Shayne listened contentedly as I read. Her eyes started to fall shut before I completed the first chapter. By the time I finished with the second, she was sound asleep.

Or so I thought, but when I moved to get out of her tiny twin bed, she woke up.

"I love you, Daddy."

"Love you, too, Doodlebug," I whispered.

"I need to kiss Mommy good night."

I got up and strode over to the framed picture that sat on the dresser and gave it to Shayne. It had been part of our routine for as long as I could remember.

Shayne trailed her small finger across the glass, over Dani's face. "I love you, Mama," she said and pressed her lips against the photo. Then, she hugged it to her chest. "Here, Daddy."

I took it from her and set it back in its place, not bothering to look at it. "Night, Doodlebug. Sleep tight."

"Don't let the bedbugs bite," she finished.

I picked up Wilbur from where he'd fallen on the floor, tucked him in beside her, and then dropped a kiss to Shayne's head. After I shut off the light, I pulled the door, making sure to leave it open a crack, and headed down the hall to my room. I closed my own door, leaned back against it, and blew out a hard breath, taking in the space.

All these years later, constant reminders of Dani lingered in this house, like secrets whispered in the dark. She had taken her last breath in this very room while I held her hand. Paving her exit from this life into the next with promises that I'd take care of Shayne, swearing that we'd be just fine. The memory, excruciating but beautiful, had always brought me some measure of comfort. Tonight though, I felt suffocated by her ghost.

6

CAMRYN

"*B*eing neighbors doesn't make us friends."

Tucker's words still echoed in my head three days later. What he'd said was the truth. We were strangers who happened to live next door to each other. Two encounters and awkwardness over brownies hadn't changed that. But why he'd felt the need to voice the thought out loud, I failed to comprehend.

I remembered the picture on his refrigerator. My heart hurt for Tucker and his daughter. So much so that I rubbed the ache in my chest. I knew what it was like to lose a parent. How deeply the scars ran when someone who was supposed to love you abandoned you. But I didn't know a damn thing about grieving the loss of someone you'd shared a life and child with.

A feeling of melancholy settled over me, and I realized, if I stayed in this house one second longer, I'd end up wasting the entire day. Next week, I'd start my new job at the elementary school, which meant that today was one of my last chances to spend a weekday doing whatever the hell I wanted, and I wanted to go to the beach.

I drank my coffee and then gathered everything I'd need for a day on the sand and in the sun. After I loaded the car, I went to my room to put on my suit.

I tied the turquoise bikini top around my neck and contorted my arms to latch the back. Goose bumps rose across my skin from the cool material. I slipped out of my panties, slid on the matching bottoms, and gave myself a once-over in the mirror. The one positive that had come out of the last few months was that I'd lost the fifteen pounds I'd been trying forever to lose. I gathered my hair into a messy bun, threw on a cover-up, grabbed my keys, and headed out the door.

There wasn't a cloud in the sky as I made the short drive to the beach. I found a parking spot with ease, and when I opened my car door, salty sea air filled my lungs. The warm sun kissed my skin, and I knew this was exactly what I needed.

Somehow, I managed to carry all my crap in one trip. My feet sank into the not-quite-scorching sand as I trudged across the beach. I scanned the area for a somewhat empty spot, and when I found it, I staked my claim. After I applied sunblock, I dropped my sunglasses into my bag and made a beeline for the ocean.

Wet sand gathered between my toes as I made my way through the shallow water. Once I was waist deep, I swam out a little way to where the waves formed. Then, I stood sideways, and when they rolled in, I would bounce up and let them carry me. The sun heated my face, and I relished in the sense of weightlessness the sea gave me.

I didn't know how long I'd spent in the water. I'd been carried out a bit, so I had to study the shoreline when I finally made my way back. My arm stretched across my forehead to block the glaring sun. I'd purposely left my sunglasses in the bag, so I wouldn't risk losing them in the water. Trying to see without them was a bitch. It took a few minutes to locate the patch of sand where I'd dropped my stuff. As I made my way along the water's edge, I heard my name, but I couldn't tell where it had come from. I walked a little further, and I heard it again. Closer this time.

"Camryn, over here."

I knew that voice. Shayne was sitting in the sand with an orange bucket, a shovel, and several Matchbox cars. I didn't see Tucker, but I was certain he was close by.

I plopped down on the beach next to her. "Hi, sweet girl. Where's your daddy?"

"Right here," came the deep voice from behind me. "I was just grabbing her sunblock." He squatted down behind Shayne and began to spray her back.

"Hey, Tucker," I greeted him and rose to my feet.

"Hi, Camryn."

"How've you been?" I asked.

"Good. And you?"

"Fine."

He didn't say anything else, so I stood there until I couldn't handle the awkwardness for another second.

"Well ... have fun, you two."

"Wait." Shayne squinted her big hazel eyes as she looked up at me. "Don't you want to build a sand castle with us?"

I'd love nothing more than to drop back to my knees alongside this precious little girl and help her build the best sand castle ever, but I wasn't sure her father would welcome the intrusion. Since Tucker made no attempt to confirm the invitation, I knew it'd be best to let it be.

"Maybe next time, sweet pea. You and your daddy have fun. Okay?"

"Okay." Shayne pouted her agreement.

"Bye, Tucker."

"Bye."

Just let it be, I reminded myself.

I grabbed a bottle of water from the cooler and downed half of it. After I reapplied sunblock, I reached into my bag and pulled out a towel. I used it to wipe my hands and then placed it over the chair before I dug back into the bag for my sunglasses and my current read. I stretched out on the lounger and opened my book.

I read a few chapters before I flipped onto my stomach and read a few more. The main character's name was Brett, and he was downright delicious. Completely lost in the story, I found myself hot and bothered in broad daylight on a public beach. So hot that I decided it was time for another swim.

I got up, dropped my book and sunglasses back into the bag, and headed toward the water. I searched the shore, hoping to catch a glimpse of Shayne and Tucker. When I failed to spot them, my eyes drifted to where they'd been earlier, but only the remnants of a sand castle remained. I walked closer and noticed the sunlight gleaming off an object. I crouched and plucked a Matchbox car from the sand, one I was pretty sure belonged to Shayne. My fingers wrapped around the toy, and I held it secure in my fist as I headed into the water. I swam for a little bit, making sure never to let go of the little car.

Before long, I decided I'd had enough sand and sea for one day, so I packed up my things and headed for home.

7

TUCKER

Shayne had crashed earlier than normal tonight. The beach had worn her out, and she'd already been asleep for a little over an hour.

After I started a load of laundry, checked in on my girl one more time, and grabbed a beer from the fridge, I headed to the back porch. With the door left open a crack to keep an ear out, I settled into one of the chairs and took a long pull from the bottle. Then, I tipped my head back, rested it against the cushion, and closed my eyes.

Visions of Camryn in her bikini swam in my head. The blue-green color was gorgeous against her light-golden skin. She had legs that went on for days. And damn those fucking curves. Staying away from her had taken every bit of resolve I possessed. Camryn was quickly becoming my kryptonite, and it was only a matter of time before desire won out.

Except for the crickets and bullfrogs, the night was quiet. Or it was until Camryn's voice drowned out everything else. It wasn't sweet like it'd been earlier when she sat beside Shayne on the beach.

"Jared, why are you calling me?" Her words were laced

7
7
7

with anger, but just underneath was something else altogether.

Who the hell is Jared?

I lifted my head a bit and looked in the direction of her house. She was pacing back and forth on her porch, holding her phone to her ear. Her porch light was on, and it was easy to make her out in the darkness.

She paused for a minute, and then she spoke again, screeching into the phone, "Are you fucking insane?"

It was evident she had no idea I was out here. My porch light wasn't on, and she hadn't even looked in my direction once.

"Listen here, you lying, cheating son of a bitch. If you think for a fucking second I'd ever be with you again, you're more delusional than I thought."

There was another pause. Longer this time and then she spoke again. The words were quieter, thicker somehow, as though she was on the verge of tears.

"Go to hell."

I heard a door slam, and I thought she'd gone inside for good until it slammed a second time. She threw herself into a chair.

"Fucking asshole," she loudly swore. "I hope his dick falls off."

I sat up and cleared my throat. "You okay?"

"Do you make it a habit to eavesdrop?"

"It was impossible not to overhear." I picked up my beer, stood, and walked to the edge of the deck. "You okay?" I asked her again.

"Fucking peachy." Her voice was thick.

I heard how hard she was trying not to cry. Whoever this Jared guy was, I wanted to beat his ass. I might not know

Camryn well, but I had the feeling that she wasn't the type of woman who cried easily.

"Want to talk about it?"

"No."

"Camryn," I pushed. I could see her, but I couldn't make out her features.

"Tucker, please, just leave me alone."

"Look, about the other night, you took me by surprise; that's all."

She didn't respond. She got up and went inside. I waited a few minutes for her to return, and when she didn't, I decided it was time to call it a night. Then, I heard her sliding glass door open, and I knew she'd come back out.

"Tucker?"

"I'm here."

I made out her frame as she walked down her stairs and onto the grass. She stumbled but caught herself.

"Ow. Shit. Damn gophers."

I went over to the door and flicked on the light. Then, I set my beer on the little plastic table Shayne used for her tea parties.

Camryn stopped near the steps that led to my deck and held something out in her palm.

I climbed down the stairs and moved to where she was.

"Here. I found this on the beach where you and Shayne built her castle. I figured it was hers." She placed a Matchbox car in my hand.

I stuck the car in the pocket of my basketball shorts. "Thank you."

Seeing her vulnerable and sad struck a chord inside me. I wanted to make it better. Erase the hurt that lined her face.

"Whoever he is, he isn't worth it."

"You're right; he isn't." She dried her face and then turned to leave. "Good night, Tucker."

"Camryn?"

She stopped, but she didn't face me. "Don't." Her breath caught.

The way she'd said the word tugged at something primal in me. I stepped closer and softly placed a large hand on her shoulder. My fingers gave a light squeeze.

"Please don't," she whispered.

I felt her body start to shake, and my chest tightened. She was on the verge of breaking down, and I couldn't force myself to walk away. Instead, I moved in front of her and hauled her into me. For a second, she struggled against my hold.

"Tucker, let me go." Her words lacked conviction.

Everything within me screamed to do as she'd asked. But this wasn't about me. Or about self-preservation. It was about her.

"Not yet."

Finally, her arms wrapped around my waist as she began to weep. Camryn's hot tears soaked through my shirt to my skin. Her body was racked with silent sobs. For whatever reason, she needed this. I knew it in the way she clung to me. How she burrowed into my chest and fisted the material covering my back. I didn't shush her or tell her it was going to be okay because I didn't know if it would be. I didn't know her story, and she didn't know mine.

This moment was all I'd ever be able to give her. It would have to be enough.

8

CAMRYN

Engulfed in his arms, I pressed my body into Tucker as close as I could get. Every emotion that I'd refused to acknowledge during the last six months spilled out of me.

Sadness. Anger. Hurt. Guilt. Loss. And, the most profound, grief.

The harder I tried to get myself under control, the faster the tears fell. Tucker never wavered. He just let me cry, and I relished his embrace. Minutes, maybe hours, passed by the time I got it together enough to form words.

When I did speak, they came out breathy and broken. "I-I'm s-sorry."

Tucker hooked a finger under my chin and drew it upward. "Don't apologize."

I dropped my arms from his waist and stepped out of his hold. "Th-thank you, Tucker. I don't think I knew how much I needed that until now." Wetness coated the palms of my hands as I dried my face.

"I'm sorry ... for whatever you went through."

I drew in a shuddered breath. "I'd better let you get back to it."

Turning away from him, I took a few steps when he called out to me, "Camryn?"

"Yeah?"

"My last name is Jaxson."

I walked back toward him, confusion etched on my swollen face. "Jaxson?"

"As in Jaxson Cove." He scuffed a hand down his beard and then crossed his arms. "There's an exhibit down at City Hall." He smirked. "And the Founder's Day Parade takes awkward to another level."

"Oh my God." A hand covered my mouth to stifle the laugh.

"I also own Jaxson's Garage, which my grandfather opened over fifty years ago."

"Wow." Hands on my hips, shocked expression in place, I said, "Your family is straight outta one of those black-and-white television shows."

"Says the women who brought over baked goods the day after she moved in."

"Touché." I crossed my arms and dropped my gaze to the ground before I continued, "Tucker ... I'm sorry. I didn't mean to—"

"You have nothing to apologize for. I'm sorry I hurt your feelings."

My eyes refused to lift until he said my name.

"Camryn, the reason I told you my last name is because it's generally something exchanged among friends."

The corners of my mouth tugged upward while I waited for him to finish.

"You were bound to find out, and it was only a matter of time before we ended up with each other's mail." He smiled. "Or you heard the old men gossiping down at McGregor's Coffee Shop."

"So, we're friends now?"

His voice dropped low. "It seems like you could use one."

He had no idea how right he was.

My smile widened. "Wait. Doesn't that make this some sort of pity friendship?"

He chuckled. "Depends on how you look at it."

"Thanks for the hug, Tucker."

"You're welcome."

"Have a good night." I headed back to my place, and before I stepped onto my porch, I called over my shoulder, "Parker."

"What?"

"My last name. It's Parker."

"Well, good night, Camryn Parker."

"Good night, Tucker Jaxson."

Later, when I climbed into bed after my shower, I lay awake for a long time, lost inside my head. My emotions swung back and forth like a pendulum. Part of me felt ashamed that I'd broken down. That I'd allowed someone else to see me in a moment of weakness. Usually, I didn't do tears. I handled whatever was thrown my way and tried like hell to move on. Tonight though, it had felt impossible. Jared had said the most awful, abhorrent things to me.

"You're not good enough. You never will be."

"Your own mother didn't even want you."

I'd tried not to let it eat away at me, but everything had come to a head. The second Tucker's hand had landed on my shoulder, I had known I was going to break. At first, when he'd tried to pull me into a hug, I'd fought against him because I knew how it would end.

Me, a sniveling mess of snot and salty tears.

Exposed. Raw. Vulnerable.

I'd never expected to find the first semblance of peace

I'd had in months in the arms of my sexy neighbor. The man who, just days ago, had seemed annoyed by my presence.

I snuggled beneath the covers, Tucker's scent clinging to my unwashed hair, and fell into a deep sleep.

9

TUCKER

Having Camryn in my arms had felt so good. Too fucking good, if I was being honest. Visions of her legs wrapped around me as I pounded into her kept me awake at night. That was why I'd been avoiding her for the last few days. Since today was the first day of school, I didn't know if it'd be possible. Hopefully, she'd be gone by the time Shayne and I left the house. Then again, there was always a chance we'd run into Camryn on campus.

My eyes shifted to the digital clock on my nightstand. I had just enough time to get ready for work before I needed to wake Shayne.

Once I was showered and dressed, I opened Shayne's bedroom door and stared at my daughter. Some kids looked angelic while they slept. Bug looked more like she'd fought off a pack of rabid dogs. Hair wild, pajama shirt bunched up around her belly, body spread eagle, covers on the floor, and one corner of the sheet undone. She was a hot mess.

I crept over to the side of her bed, gently pushed her leg out of the way, and sat down. My fingers brushed across her forehead, smoothing out the creases. I planted a kiss on the tip of her nose and whispered, "Doodlebug, it's time to wake up."

Her eyes fluttered open. "Nope. I'm still sleeping," she said and rolled onto her side.

"Okay, but you're going to be late on your first day of school."

"School is today?" She shot straight up, wide-eyed, nearly head-butting me in the process.

"It is."

She squealed and scrambled into my lap, her hands planted on my cheeks. "Daddy! This is going to be the best day ever."

I pulled her into a hug. "It is, Bug, but you need to get dressed."

"I know exactly what I'm going to wear."

"One of the new outfits Grammy bought you this weekend?"

She looked thoughtful. "Yes, but not the one with flowers on it. I'm not about that life."

I laughed and lifted her off my lap. "All right. Hurry up, and I'll go make you breakfast."

"Chocolate chip pancakes?" she asked, hopeful.

I looked at my watch and raised an eyebrow at her. "Not today, kiddo. You'll have to settle for a chocolate chip Eggo."

"Frozen waffles are a travesty."

"You're too much." I laughed again. The kid cracked me up. "Come on, enough goofing off. Get dressed. I'm driving you to school today."

"When do I start riding the bus?"

"Tomorrow."

"And they'll pick me up from the shop before school and drop me off after, right?"

"Yes."

We'd been over this a dozen times in the last few days, but I knew she was still nervous.

"Get a move on," I told her as I walked out of the room.

Back in the kitchen, I poured coffee into a large to-go mug and dropped a waffle into the toaster. I grabbed Shayne a juice box from the pantry while I waited for her breakfast.

"How do I look?" Shayne asked from the kitchen doorway. She was wearing a pair of denim shorts with a shirt that read *Sassy Pants* across it.

"Beautiful. Let's go fix your hair."

I followed behind her as she led the way to the bathroom.

She pulled out one of the drawers, withdrew a brush and hair tie, and then gave them to me. "Can you braid it?"

"We don't have time, baby." I ran the brush through her strands before gathering it into a perfect ponytail. It had taken a hell of a lot of practice and patience, but thanks to my mom and a few YouTube videos, I'd figured it out. "All right, brush your teeth and meet me in the kitchen."

In less than two minutes, Shayne was back and seated at the table. I put her breakfast in front of her, and she suspiciously eyed it.

She picked it up to inspect the other side. "Daddy, it's burned."

Burned was an exaggeration. Really brown? Yes, but not burned. We didn't have time for me to make another one.

"Hang on."

I took it off her plate, reached into the silverware drawer for a butter knife, and then walked over to the sink. The knife scraped against the little squares until fine charcolored crumbs dusted the sink. I held it up. For good measure, I blew across the surface. Perfect.

I turned back to Shayne. "See? All better." I wrapped the

abused waffle in a paper towel and then gave it to her. "You'll have to eat in the truck, Bug. We need to go."

"All right."

It took some maneuvering, but we finally made it outside with everything we needed, including Bug's backpack and my coffee. Shayne ate her breakfast and talked nonstop on the way to school. I was glad she was excited because it made me leaving her a whole lot easier. When we finally made it in the front of the school, I parked on the grass. There was no way I wasn't going to walk her to class. I took a drink of my coffee and placed it in the cupholder.

"Ready, Doodlebug?" I asked, looking at my girl.

"Let's do this."

I got out of the truck and went around to get her out. Together, we slid on her backpack and made our way to the sidewalk. Shayne's small hand held firmly to my larger one. As we passed by the front office, she pulled from my grasp.

"Camryn!" Shayne yelled and made a beeline for her.

Camryn stood off to the side with a huge smile on her face. Her hair cascaded in waves down her back. Dressed in jeans and a flowy shirt, she was beautiful. When she bent to scoop Shayne into a hug, my chest tightened.

I closed the space between us. "Hey. How've you been?"

She seemed a little flustered, and it took a minute for her to find her voice. It made me wonder if I was affecting her the same way that I didn't want to admit she was affecting me.

"Good." She cleared her throat and stood. "What about you?"

"Busy." It wasn't an excuse.

"Are you ready for your first day?" Camryn asked Shayne.

"I sure am. Daddy's walking me to class."

Shayne looked around at all the kids as they walked past, and I saw the moment the smile slipped from her face. Many of the other children were with both their parents, and in that moment, my heart broke for my little girl.

"Doodlebug, tell Miss Parker good-bye."

"Who's Miss Parker?"

"Me, silly," Camryn told her. "You can call me Camryn when we aren't at school, but at school, I have to be Miss Parker. Okay?"

"Okay." Shayne looked thoughtful. "Camryn? Oops. I mean, Miss Parker. Do you think you could walk with me and my dad to my classroom?"

"Um ..." Camryn looked like a deer caught in the headlights.

Our eyes met, and I knew she was asking me if it was okay.

For Shayne, there would always be moments like this. Times when she wanted her mom, needed someone to fill that role for her. Situations when she'd feel left out because her mom was gone. If she wanted Camryn to stand in the gap on the first day of school, I wasn't going to say no because this wasn't about me. I gave Camryn a nod of approval.

"If it's okay with your daddy," Camryn agreed.

Even though she knew my answer, I appreciated that she'd deferred to me anyway.

Shayne looked up at me with hopeful eyes, ones that were the same color as my own. "Daddy, is it okay?"

"Sure, Bug. Let's go."

She slipped one small hand into mine and the other into Camryn's as we joined in with the crowd. I ignored the hurt deep inside my chest. Dani should've been here for this, and she wasn't the only one. There were moments in my life where, even though things felt right, they were all kinds of wrong. This was one of those moments.

"We're here," I said when we arrived outside of Mrs. Jenkins's classroom.

I knelt to be eye-level with Shayne. She released Camryn's hand and wrapped both her arms around my neck.

She squeezed me tight and whispered against my ear, "I love you so much, Daddy."

"I love you, too, Bug," I whispered back. "More than anything in the world."

"Tucker, do you have your phone?" Camryn asked.

I looked around and noticed the other parents holding up their phones. "Yeah," I told her and took it out of my pocket.

"Want me to take it for you?" Camryn offered.

"That would be great." I passed her my phone.

"All right, you two, let me see big smiles."

Still in my kneeling position, I tucked Shayne into my side, and we smiled for the picture.

"Aw, you two look great." Camryn snapped the photo and then held out the phone to me.

I stood, but before I could take it from her, Shayne interjected, "Wait. Can we take one of the three of us?"

It was a horrible idea. Camryn had been dominating my thoughts lately. The last thing I needed was an image of her on my phone.

I can always delete it later, I rationalized. *We'll take one to appease Shayne, and then I'll erase it.*

Even as the thought entered my head, I knew it was a lie.

"Do you mind?" I asked, directing the question to Camryn.

"Not at all," she conceded, but from the look on her face, she thought it was as bad of an idea as I did.

I took the phone from her, and we all squeezed into the frame. Shayne's smile was full blown and genuine. Camryn's looked as uncertain as my own.

When the bell rang, I turned to Shayne. "All right, it's that time. I'll pick you up after school."

"Okay." She wrapped her arms around my waist, and I dropped a kiss to the top of her head.

Mrs. Jenkins stood at the classroom door, reassuring parents as she ushered in their kids.

Shayne was a bit reluctant, but she detached herself from around me and walked inside the classroom.

I turned away and headed back the way we had come, so I could leave. Camryn fell in step beside me.

"Thank you. For what you did for Shayne." I shoved my hands into the pockets of my jeans.

"Tucker, it wasn't a big deal."

"It was a very big deal to her." To me, too, but she didn't need to know that.

"Well, you're welcome."

"Have a great first day, Miss Parker," I said as we approached the corner where we'd found her earlier.

"See you, Tucker."

I offered her a smile before I walked back to my truck and drove to work. When I arrived at the garage, Nash looked up as I walked into the lobby.

"Good morning," I addressed the few clients that sat, waiting for their cars.

"Hey, slacker. Nice of you to show up." Nash loved nothing more than to give me shit. We'd been friends since we were kids. "Did you enjoy your vacation?"

"We did."

"Shayne get off to school okay?"

"Yep. She was a little nervous but handled it like a champ." I walked behind the counter and flipped through the appointment book. We had a computer program to track everything, but the book was easier, and it didn't crash. "Looks like it's going to be a busy day."

"You can say that again."

"All right, I'm going to go change, and I'll be out there in a few," I told him as I made my way into my office.

"Wait up," Nash called after me.

I faced him and raised a brow.

He stepped around me. I knew that look. Without prompting, I closed the door, crossed my arms, and waited for him to speak.

"Did you hear Holly was back in town?"

"We ran into each other at the bar last week, but since you're asking, I assume you know that."

"I might've heard. You good?"

"So, what? You want to stand around and talk about feelings and shit now?"

"Just checkin', man." He threw his hands up in surrender.

Frustrated, I reached up to grip my hair and looked at Nash. "I'm fine, and we aren't going to talk about it."

"Tuck, it's been years, man. When are you going to let it go?"

I glared at him. "Really, Nash? You want to go there? I give zero fucks about Holly. I have let it go. I don't want to talk about her, and I don't want to see her."

"No worries there, my friend. She's already gone."

"Well, thank God for small favors," I said, relieved.

"Look, I know—"

"Nash." It was a warning, and he damn well knew it.

"Fine." He crossed his arms. "How's that new next-door neighbor of yours?"

A smile crept over my face before I could stop it.

"Damn, Tuck." He smirked. "Macy was right."

"Right about what?"

"Nothing, man." He dropped his eyes and looked anywhere but at me.

"Nash, are you forgetting who signs your fucking paycheck?"

"Not cool, bro. Not at all."

My gaze turned hard.

"Please tell me you don't think your new neighbor moved into that house by accident."

Leave it to Macy to stick her damn nose in my business. "Macy is a pain in my ass."

"Mine, too, man."

"When the hell are you two going to get your heads out of your asses?"

His jaw tensed. "Not going there, man."

Nash and Macy had been together off and on since we were kids. For some reason, as adults, neither one of them had managed to get their shit together.

"All right. Then, shut up and get your ass back to work."

He raised a hand in mock salute. "Yes, sir, boss." Nash opened the door and then pulled it shut behind him.

Asshole. He knew I hated when he called me that.

After I had taken over the garage, I'd made a few upgrades, including adding a private bathroom with a small shower and a custom armoire, built to resemble an upright toolbox, where I kept extra clothes.

I changed, made sure the coffee in the lobby was fresh, and went out to help my crew service the cars. We were so busy that I worked straight through lunch. A while later, covered in sweat and grease, it was time to go pick up my girl.

"Nash, I'm out, but I'll be back."

We still had three brake jobs, a few tire rotations, and a transmission install to finish up before we closed at six.

"All right, man. See you in a bit."

The garage might not be the ideal place for a kid to hang out, but Shayne was used to it.

When she was younger, on the days my mom couldn't watch her, she'd hung out at the shop. There was a dedicated corner of my office just for her, though the space had transitioned over the years according to Shayne's age. With a small television and enough toys and art supplies to keep her busy for an hour or two, Shayne was happy. Being a single parent with a business to run meant I did whatever the hell I needed to make it work. Lucky for me, being the boss had its perks.

10

CAMRYN

Aside from a few of the younger students who came to the office, complaining of a stomachache that had more to do with separation anxiety than actual illness, the first day of school had been uneventful. That meant I'd had plenty of time to think of Tucker and Shayne.

This morning, she'd surprised me when she asked if I'd walk with them to her classroom. I was even more shocked when Tucker agreed. But I saw it. That brief second he'd allowed his mask to slip. The raw emotion he worked hard to conceal written all over his face. Unspoken longing for the woman who should've been here with them, holding their daughter's hand and snapping selfies. Sadness gripped my insides. I'd hurt for both of them, and I'd wanted nothing more than to gather Tucker and Shayne into my arms for a hug. To be there for them in the same way Tucker had been for me the other night.

The dismissal bell rang, effectively pulling me from my thoughts. Since it was the first day of school, I had car duty with the rest of the staff. I stepped out from the designated nurse's station and made my way toward the front of the school. Children sat crisscross on the sidewalk behind a painted yellow line. As I made my way through the throng of sweaty faces, I was careful not to step on any limbs or fingers that darted beyond the safe zone. I'd been assigned to the kindergarten and first grade section, so I scanned the sea of faces for the little girl who was quickly becoming my favorite person.

Shayne must have felt my eyes on her because she stopped talking to the boy who sat beside her and looked at me. Her face morphed into the biggest smile, and she thrust her small hand into the air to wave. I returned the gesture, and then she went back to talking with her young friend.

I focused my attention to the street where cars were lined up, waiting to turn into the school. Mr. Rogers, our principal, stood in the middle of the asphalt semicircle, headset mic in place. The sun was beating down, and wetness pooled on the back of his baby-blue dress shirt, which caused the material to stick to him. Florida in August was comparative to the seventh ring of hell, and hopefully, we'd be able to get the children loaded into their respective vehicles before we all died of heatstroke.

Card-stock signs bearing children's names were either hanging from rearview mirrors or pressed against windshields. As Mr. Rogers called off the names of students, he directed parents to the appropriate spot.

"Shayne Jaxson," he said into the mic.

Shayne stood, and I held out a hand to help her step around her classmates. "Did you have a good day?"

"I did. Mrs. Jenkins is so nice. And I made a friend. Oh, and we have a class pet. I'll get—"

"How about you tell me all about it later? Your dad's here." I pointed to Tucker's black truck. As he pulled up to the curb, I opened the rear passenger door.

"Hey, Doodlebug," he greeted Shayne. "Hi, Camryn."

"Hi, Daddy. We're still at school, so you have to call her Miss Parker, remember?"

I laughed. "It's all right, Shayne. Can you buckle in, or do you need help?"

"I've got it, but thank you."

"Thanks, Miss Parker." Tucker smirked.

And damn if I didn't find it sensual as hell. I'd heard the expression *sex on a stick*. Read it at least a dozen times in romance novels. An overused cliché that seemed more fucking ridiculous every time I came across it. That was before Tucker Jaxson. The relaxed way he sat behind the wheel—elbow bent, hand positioned at twelve o'clock, sweaty from manual labor—that phrase was exactly what came to mind. A woman could get off from the arm porn alone. Especially if you took the streak of grease that marked his bicep into consideration.

"You can shut the door. I'm snug as a bug." Shayne yanked on her seat belt. "See?"

Embarrassment painted my cheeks, but somehow, I managed to string words together. "Ah, look at that. Snug as a bug indeed. Have a good night, you two," I told them without making eye contact and shut the door. Then, I berated myself over the forgotten sunglasses in my car because I desperately wanted something to hide behind.

It took more than twenty minutes to get the rest of the students loaded up to go home. After a quick chat with the school secretary about how the first day had gone, I gathered my belongings and got ready to head out.

The first two weeks of school passed rather quickly, and

while I saw Shayne here and there on campus, I hadn't seen Tucker—at least, not at school. We would see each other in passing but didn't talk much beyond that. It didn't stop my thoughts from being consumed by him. The attraction I felt was undeniable. It wasn't something I intended to act on. Tucker offered me friendship, and as far as friends went, I didn't have many of those. The past several months had been rough, and right now, I could use one.

Sexual frustration wasn't something my vibrator or a swim in the ocean couldn't handle. It had been a bit since my last trip to the beach, and the thought of a hard swim sounded fantastic. Since I didn't have any other plans, now seemed as good a time as any.

After I threw a bag together, I slid into the driver's seat, rolled down my window, and stuck the key in the ignition. When I turned it, Lucille made an awful noise. My head dropped onto the steering wheel.

"Whatcha doin'?"

The sound of Shayne's voice made me jump.

"Shayne, you scared the crap out of me." I pressed a hand over my heart.

"Oh, you said crap," she singsonged and covered her mouth. Her long brown hair was in low pigtails, Tucker's ball cap perched backward on her head. She wore a black tank top, which had white powder on it, and a pair of pink shorts with pineapples on them.

"Sorry," I said, though I was sure she'd heard worse.

"I'm just kidding. Crap isn't really a bad word. At least you didn't say shit."

I was so stunned that I could only laugh. "I was worried there for a minute." She wasn't my kid, which meant it wasn't my place to correct her. "Hey, Shayne, did you have powdered doughnuts for breakfast?"

"Yep. Why are you sitting here?" She waved her index finger between me and the steering wheel. "Are you sad?"

"A little. I think Lucille is broken."

"Oh no! That's horrible. Um, who's Lucille again?"

"My car."

"You named your car? I thought only boys did that."

"Yes, Lucille is my car, and I'm pretty sure she's broken."

"I'm sorry, but don't be sad. I bet my daddy can fix it."

Just then, Tucker's voice came across the lawn. "Shayne!"

"Over here, Daddy." She frantically waved her arm.

"Watch out, sweet girl. I'm going to open the door."

Shayne moved, and I got out of the car.

Tucker came to a stop in front of us. "Good morning, Camryn." He folded his arms over his broad chest. The black T-shirt he wore pulled taut over his muscled arms.

It should be illegal to look that damn good.

"'Morning, Tucker."

He directed his attention to Shayne. "I thought you were supposed to be watching cartoons while I was in the shower."

"I was, but then I got bored, and I asked you if I could come outside to play on the porch. You said yes really loud through the bathroom door."

Tucker tilted his head skyward and muttered something under his breath that I couldn't quite make out. If I didn't know better, I'd think he was embarrassed.

He scuffed a hand over his face and then knelt to get on Shayne's level. "Bug, next time, just wait until I get out of the shower. You aren't allowed to go outside by yourself. You're only five."

"But I'm almost six, and I wasn't by myself." She pointed a finger at me.

My teeth bit into my lip to hide the grin that threatened

to escape. I was pretty sure she had a bright future as a criminal defense attorney. One who specialized in getting her clients off on technicalities.

"That's not the point, Shayne. Never again. Do you understand?" His tone was firm, but he didn't raise his voice.

"I'm sorry, Daddy." She tightly hugged him and then pulled back to see his face. "Lucille is broken."

He looked at her, puzzled. "Who's Lucille?"

"Camryn's car. And guess what else? Camryn is a witch."

"Shayne, that's not nice."

"I don't mean it in a bad way. I just mean, she's magic. She knew I had powdered doughnuts for breakfast."

Tucker laughed, and I joined in.

"That's because you have the powder all over your shirt," I told her.

"Aw, man. I was hoping you were really magic."

"Sorry to disappoint you, kiddo."

"That's all right."

Tucker rose to his full height and met my eyes. "Car trouble again? Ever think about getting a new one?"

His words struck a nerve. He had no way of knowing how much my car meant to me. To some, it didn't seem like a lot, but to me, Lucille was everything. Something in my expression must've made Tucker aware there was more to it than that.

He placed a hand on my shoulder. "I'm just giving you a hard time." He squeezed gently and then dropped his hand. "Tell me what's going on."

"It needs a tune-up, and I've been putting it off. It won't start, and I'm pretty sure it isn't the battery this time." Not that I needed to remind him of that.

"I'll have a look. Pop the hood."

"See? I told you Daddy could fix it," Shayne chimed in.

"Tucker, you don't have to do that. I can have it towed to the shop."

Tucker's eyes met mine for a brief second. Then, he stepped around me, leaned in close, and whispered, "Let me help you." His warm breath danced across my skin. He was too close and not close enough.

Without waiting for permission, he opened my car door and pulled the hood release. Then, he turned the key that was still in the ignition.

Shayne's hands went to her ears when the car tried to kick over. "Yep, she's broken."

Tucker turned the ignition off and walked around to the front of the car. He unlatched the hood and peered inside the engine compartment. "I'm going to go grab some tools from the house. I'll be right back." He looked at Shayne. "Are you going to hang with Camryn for a second or come with me?"

She glanced up at me. "Can I hang with you?"

"You sure can, sweet girl."

Shayne and I entertained ourselves by telling knock-knock jokes until Tucker returned a few minutes later, carrying a toolbox.

"I'm positive it's your alternator, but I'm going to check to be sure." He set the metal box on the ground.

I knew alternators weren't cheap, but it could be a lot worse. "Thanks for doing this, Tucker. I appreciate it."

"It's no problem." He wiped sweat from his brow and then looked at Shayne. "Hey, Doodlebug, you want to help?"

"I get to be your assistant?" She punched a fist into the air and brought her arm down. "Yes."

"Okay, grab the voltage meter from the toolbox."

Shayne flipped the metal latch and opened the lid. It made a clanking sound when it smacked the concrete.

"Here, Daddy." She held up the plastic rectangle and placed it in Tucker's palm.

I couldn't hide my surprise. "Wow. She really knows her stuff."

"Daddy teaches me a lot about cars," she proudly declared.

"I can see that. My dad taught me about cars, too."

Tucker looked up from his task and raised a questioning brow.

"I know how to change a tire, and I can even change the oil," I imitated Shayne's tone.

"Impressive." He wrapped the wire back around the meter box. "Here, Bug, put this back, please."

He gave it to her, and she did as she had been asked.

Then, Shayne busied herself, playing on the lawn and attempting cartwheels.

Tucker grazed my arm to get my attention. The split second of contact caused goose bumps to rise on my skin.

"You need a new alternator. It's not charging the battery; that's why it won't start."

Mentally, I recalled the balance of my bank account and how much cash I had on hand. "Any idea how much that's going to run?" I tried to keep the concern from my voice. Lucille needed more than an alternator, and I was well aware of it.

"You need new spark plugs and wires, too. Ballpark? About three hundred."

That was doable.

"All right, I'll see about getting it towed to your garage."

"Why would you do that? I'll just run into town for the parts and fix it here."

"Tucker, I can't let you do that."

72

He folded those glorious arms across his chest. "Why not?"

"Because it makes me feel like I'm taking advantage of you."

"You're not." He took a step forward, getting in my personal space. "I offered. Besides, I'm not sure when my guys could get to it. We've been slammed this past week. I'm off today, which means I can fix it here. It'll take a few hours, but you'll have your car for work on Monday."

"Are you sure? You really don't have to do this."

"I know I don't have to. And, yes, I'm sure. I wouldn't have suggested it otherwise."

"All right, but you have to let me pay you."

"Not happening."

Arguing with him had proven to be pointless so far, but I wasn't going to go down without a fight.

"Tucker, if you're going to spend practically an entire day working on my car and you refuse to let me pay you ... at least let me make dinner for you and Shayne."

He looked thoughtful for a minute, as though considering it. "Well ... that depends."

"On?"

"Can you cook?"

"Of course I can cook." I laughed.

"A woman who can change her own oil and cook? Damn." He raised a brow. "You've got yourself a deal."

11

TUCKER

Camryn's laughter hit my ears and sent a jolt to my cock. And that smile? It took my fucking breath away. Every time I was in her presence, I wanted more.

An errant strand of hair escaped her ponytail and blew across her face. Without a second thought, I reached for it and tucked it behind her ear. For a brief second, she leaned into my palm, and my touch lingered for an instant longer than was appropriate. I was headed into dangerous territory.

I dropped my hand, and we stared at each other for several beats. Camryn's tongue darted out, licking her perfect pink bottom lip. My dick was already halfway hard, and after that little move right there, it took every ounce of restraint I had to keep from bending her over the hood of her car. Except I couldn't do that for several reasons, not the least of them being that my daughter was feet away, playing in the grass.

"All right, I need to get to work on this."

"I should go change clothes. I'll be right back," Camryn said.

A better man would have turned his attention to the task

at hand. My eyes stayed glued to her as she walked inside. She had on this little dress-looking thing over her swimsuit that hit about an inch below her ass cheeks. *Damn.*

When she closed the door, I glanced over to Shayne and then got to work on the alternator.

A few minutes later, Camryn returned with three red plastic cups. "Here, I brought you some lemonade."

She held out the cup, and I nodded my thanks. She'd changed into a pair of shorts and a V-neck tank top that pulled my eyes straight to the valley between her tits.

"I'm going to hang out with your kid."

I watched as she walked over to Shayne, offering her one of the cups. She said something to Shayne that I couldn't quite make out. Camryn set her drink on the ground, and the next thing I knew, she was taking off at a run. She completed a perfect cartwheel, flung herself into the air, and landed on her feet. It was sexy as hell.

And that dangerous territory? I was already fucking there.

12

CAMRYN

I closed the door behind me and leaned against it.

Tucker and Shayne had just left to head into town for parts. I'd given him the cash I had on hand, which should cover the costs. He'd invited me to go along, but I'd told him I wanted to start dinner. He had given me a strange look, but the truth was, I needed a few minutes alone to pull my shit together.

Tucker Jaxson ignited all my nerve endings. Not only was he gorgeous, but also the way he was with his daughter only made him that much more attractive. If I didn't put a little bit of space between us, I was convinced I'd spontaneously combust.

I moved away from the door and went into the kitchen to start prepping the spaghetti sauce. Nonna had taught me to make it when I was younger. I'd been feeling nostalgic earlier this week when I went to the market, so I'd picked up the ingredients to make a few of her recipes. She was the closest thing I'd had to a mom since mine had left around my third birthday. Nonna had passed a few years ago, but making her dishes always made me feel close to her.

After I gathered the makings to prep the sauce, I lost myself in the mundane tasks of chopping, grating, dicing, and sautéing. The kitchen filled with the enticing aroma of the flavors marrying together, the scent so familiar that I felt like a little girl again. I put the remaining ingredients in and then transferred the sauce to the Crock-Pot.

Before I had a chance to start the rest of the chores I'd let slide this week, my phone alerted me to a new email. I wiped my hands and grabbed my cell off the counter.

To: Camryn
From: Grayson
Re: Subject: New contact info
Hey, gorgeous. Congrats on the new job. It's been a few weeks. Hope all is well. Does your new place have an extra bedroom? I'm thinking about coming back to the States soon. I'll be in touch.
Lots of love,
G

I typed out a quick reply.

To: Grayson
From: Camryn
Re: Re: Subject: New contact info
Tired of Europe already? I always have room for you. Come visit me.
Miss you,
C

Grayson was the one friendship I'd made that stuck, and even though it'd been a couple of years since we'd seen each other, we'd remained close despite the distance. A visit was long overdue, and I hoped like hell it would happen soon.

I set my phone on the counter and went to deal with the laundry. I just finished putting it away when a knock sounded on the door. I went to answer it and found Tucker and Shayne on the other side. His arms were weighted down with bags.

"What's all this? Is there more? Do you need help?" I opened the door wide and stood out of the way to allow them to enter.

"I picked up lunch on the way back. I wasn't sure what you wanted, so I stopped at our favorite Chinese place and got a little bit of everything." He walked into my kitchen with Shayne on his heels.

"Thanks. I haven't had good Chinese food in forever." I went to the cabinet, grabbed paper plates, and set them on the island.

Tucker emptied the bags, placing the assorted takeout containers on the counter.

"Something smells yummy," Shayne said.

"It's the homemade spaghetti sauce."

"I love spaghetti."

I looked at Tucker. "What do you want to drink? I have lemonade, water, sweet tea, and beer."

Shayne chewed on the end of her straw. "Daddy already bought me a drink."

"I see that." I smiled at her and turned to Tucker.

"Beer would be great."

I grabbed two beers from the fridge, opened them, and passed one to Tucker. I watched his Adam's apple bob while he chugged half of it. I'd love to trace my tongue over his stubble. Feel the roughness against my lips. Tucker's heated gaze landed on mine, as though he could read my thoughts. He pulled the bottle from his mouth and smirked at me. He was sexy, and he damn well knew exactly what he did to me.

My face flushed because I'd been caught checking him out. To hide my embarrassment, I turned away to focus my attention on Shayne.

She stood by one of the barstools at the island.

"Do you need some help, or can you climb up by yourself?"

"I can do it," she said. Her drink wobbled as she stretched to set it on the countertop. She tugged at the stool and nearly sent it toppling over.

"Here, let me pull it out for you."

She used the support bar on the bottom to boost herself up, and then she squirmed her way onto the seat. I carefully watched her, ready to catch her if I needed to. It took her a minute, but she finally righted herself, and I scooted her stool up to the ledge.

While I was helping her get seated, Tucker made Shayne a plate of white rice and sweet and sour chicken. He reached for a pair of chopsticks that were banded at the top and laid them on the edge of her plate. Cautiously, he set it in front of her before filling another dish with food. He wasn't kidding when he'd said he ordered a little bit of everything. He passed the plate to me before he served himself.

My eyes were fixed on him.

"What?" he asked.

"You made my plate." The surprise was evident in my voice.

"Why wouldn't I?"

"I don't know. It's just ... nothing. Never mind. Um ... thank you."

Tucker was considerate. It wasn't something I was accustomed to, and he probably thought I was insane. I sat next to Shayne and opened my chopsticks.

"You're welcome." Tucker sat on the other side of his daughter.

"Daddy, can I have my fortune cookie?"

"You have to eat first."

"Okay." She used the chopsticks like a sword, speared her chicken, and ate it.

I couldn't help the smile that spread over my face. "Do you want a fork?" I asked her.

"No, thank you. I'm resourceful."

"How are you going to eat your rice though?"

"Like this," she said. Her small fingers moved the sticks, and she scooped rice into her mouth. "See," she said, her mouth full.

"Bug, don't talk with your mouth full," Tucker chided.

"You are resourceful. That's a big word for such a little girl," I told her.

"I know lots of big words."

"What's your favorite?"

She looked thoughtful. "Exasperating."

"That's a good one," I told her.

"Yep. Daddy says it all the time. He says, 'Bug, sometimes, you're exasperating.'" She dropped her voice low to mimic her father's, and we all busted out laughing.

Tucker ruffled Shayne's hair. "You're the best, Bug."

"So are you, Daddy."

I swooned so damn hard. The more scenes like this I witnessed made me realize it would only be a matter of time before I lost my heart. The thought terrified me.

We finished eating, and Tucker was the first one to get up. "I'm going to get to work. It's pretty hot out. Do you mind if she hangs in here with you?"

"Of course not. We'll find something fun to do." I smiled at Shayne.

Tucker threw his plate away and washed his hands at the kitchen sink. He turned to Shayne and spoke, "I'll be right outside if you need me. Listen to Camryn, okay?"

Shayne let out a yawn. "Okay, Daddy."

When Tucker walked out the door, I turned to Shayne. "Looks like it's just me and you, kiddo." I got up to throw my plate away.

"I'm done," she said, holding out her plate. "Can I have my cookie now?"

She had eaten most of her food though not all of it.

"Sure." I discarded her trash and set the pile of fortune cookies in front of her. Her eyes widened, and I laughed. "You can pick one."

Shayne assessed the wrapped cellophane packages before choosing one. "Will you open it for me?"

I did as she'd asked and handed it back to her.

She broke it open and pulled out the slip of paper. "Um, I can't read all of these words."

"You can read some of them?"

"Yes. Grammy bought me flash cards, and Daddy teaches me big words when we read. It's in the rules." She'd said it like there was a list.

This was the second time she'd mentioned the rules, so I asked, "What rules?"

"Mom rules."

I didn't want to press her further, but my curiosity was piqued.

"So, are you going to read it to me?"

I took the slip of paper from her and read, "*In life, the little things are the big things.*"

Confusion played over her little features. "What does that even mean?"

"It means that little things are what really matter. Not

fancy houses or fast cars, but the way wildflowers smell and hugs and kisses and making memories."

"And bedtime stories?"

"Definitely bedtime stories. And dancing in the rain."

"That sounds fun. Daddy never lets me dance in the rain. He says, 'Bug, lightning is dangerous.'" She did that thing with her voice again to mimic Tucker's.

I laughed because it never got old. "How about we clean up the kitchen and put away the food? Then, we'll find something fun to do."

"Okay, but I'm stuck."

I realized she was right. I went over to her, pulled out the barstool, and helped her leap down. Together, we restored order in the kitchen, and then I took her into the bathroom. I opened the drawer that housed my collection of nail polish.

Shayne's eyes went wide. "Wow! It looks like a rainbow threw up in there."

"It sure does." I laughed. "Pick out whatever color you want." While she did that, I opened another drawer, applied some lip balm, and dropped it back inside.

"Can I pick two colors? Then, we can make a pattern. And what about my toes? Can we paint those, too?"

"Sure."

"Yes!" She made a fist and punched the air. "This is going to be so fun."

Shayne picked out her polish while I gathered the nail file, cotton balls, and polish remover. I turned on the warm water and grabbed a washcloth from the linen closet, dampening it. I squeezed out the excess and gave it to Shayne.

"What's this for?" she asked.

"To wipe off your hands and feet."

"Good idea."

We made our way back to the living room, and I set our supplies on the chest that served as a makeshift coffee table. After I grabbed a few paper towels and a paper plate from the kitchen, I returned to the couch.

I took the polish from Shayne's hands, setting them aside, and then I reached for her hand. I wiped one and then the other before I helped her out of her boots and repeated the process with her feet.

"That tickles," she shrieked and wiggled her toes.

"My feet are ticklish, too." I smiled. "Are you ready?"

"Yes. Can we do my toes first?"

"Of course. What color do you want to start with?"

"Um ... blue."

Her excitement over something so simple made me think of what it would be like to have a daughter of my own.

Shayne leaned back against the arm of the couch, and I gently tugged her foot toward me, propping it up on my leg. After I tore a few cotton balls into smaller pieces, I rolled them and placed the soft material between her toes to separate them.

With the bottle held securely in my hand, I twisted off the cap. "Hold real still, okay?"

"I will. Grammy paints my nails sometimes. I have to be a statue." She was quiet for a few minutes before she asked, "Did your mommy paint your nails?"

Her innocent question caused a deep ache in my chest. I never thought about my mother much. A woman who had abandoned her family because she didn't want to be a mom or wife anymore didn't deserve consideration.

"I didn't have a mommy."

"But everybody has a mommy. Even me. Except she died when I was really little."

"I'm sorry, sweet girl."

"It's okay. I don't remember her. Daddy shows me pictures though and tells me stories about her. They were best friends."

I wasn't sure how Tucker would feel about her telling me the intimate details of their lives, but she was five, and a lot of times, kids didn't have filters.

I didn't know what to say, so I told her the truth. "My mom left when I was a little girl."

"Your mommy died, too?"

"No," I answered while I reached for her other foot and more pieces of cotton. "She decided she didn't want to be a mommy anymore, so she left me with my dad and never came back."

Shayne's eyes filled with sadness, and she sat up a little. Her small hand touched my arm. "Camryn, I'm sorry your mommy didn't want you."

Her words hit me straight in the heart. The truth still hurt.

"It's okay, Shayne," I assured her. "I had my Nonna."

"What's a Nonna?"

"Nonna is what I called my grandma."

"I get it. You had Nonna like I have Grammy."

"Exactly."

"What happen to your Nonna?"

I'd had enough talk of death and loss. Our game of twenty questions had taken a turn, and I was desperate to change the subject.

"What do you think?" I held her feet up a tiny bit.

"They look so cool."

"I'm glad you like them. Ready for your fingers?"

I slid her feet off my lap, and she moved closer to me. Her toes grazed the table.

"Oh, man. I jacked my polish."

"Jacked?" I laughed. She sounded like an adult in a kid's body.

"Yep. That's what Daddy says when something gets messed up. Can you fix it?"

"I sure can. Want to give me that bottle right there?" I pointed to the acetone.

She leaned forward, grabbed the bottle with both hands, and then gave it to me. I twisted off the cap and dampened a cotton ball. Then, I wiped the polish off her big toe and repainted it.

"There." I placed the soiled cotton on the paper plate and started on her fingernails.

"Thank you for fixing it."

"You're welcome. You're so polite."

"Daddy says I have to have manners. It's in the rules, too."

While I painted her fingernails, I made certain to steer the conversation toward lighter topics. Since she had to sit still while we waited for her nails to dry, she asked me if I'd read her a story. I went to my bedroom to grab *The Lion, the Witch and the Wardrobe* off my shelf and carried it back into the living room.

I sat on the end of the couch and opened the book, and when Shayne nestled into my side, I put my arm around her and began to read. I was so wrapped up in the story, I hadn't noticed that Shayne had fallen asleep. Or that Tucker was standing in the doorway, watching me.

13

TUCKER

Camryn's car was being a pain in my ass, but it wasn't anything I couldn't handle. However, the blood that dripped down my hand didn't help matters. I grabbed a shop towel, wrapped it over the gash, and then opened Camryn's front door.

Camryn was reading while my little girl was curled into her side, sleeping peacefully. The sight nearly took my breath away. I knew the minute Camryn felt my eyes on her. Her gaze lifted, and then her eyes went wide.

"What did you do?" she whispered and gestured to my hand.

"Nothing. It's just a little scratch." I closed the door behind me.

Carefully, she lifted Shayne from against her, so she could get up. She slipped a small pillow in place and then gently laid Shayne's head on it before walking over to me.

She reached for me and unwrapped the thick paper towel to inspect it before covering it back. There was a good two-inch gash on top of my hand, just below my knuckles.

"Just a scratch, my ass. Come on, I'll get you cleaned up."

I followed her down the hall and to the bathroom.

She stepped out of the way, so I could enter.

"Wash your hands."

I unwrapped the soiled cloth and placed it in the waste-basket. Then, I turned on the water and squirted some antibacterial soap into my palms.

Camryn opened the small closet, withdrew a clean towel, and set it on the sink. She took my hand and held it under the stream of water. Her delicate fingers moved tenderly over my skin, angling the wound to remove the dirt. Normally, I wiped the blood on my jeans and kept going, but I knew this cut was deep enough to at least warrant washing. Still, I wouldn't have gone to the trouble to be so thorough. I didn't stop her because I liked the feel of her hands on me. Enjoyed the way she made a fuss. It had been a long time since someone did that for me.

Camryn's eyes met mine as she shut off the water and reached for the towel to wrap over my hand. Tenderly, she patted it dry. She was close. Close enough that I breathed in her orange blossom and honey scent.

I wanted to touch her. Brush my lips against her mouth. She made me want to break all my self-imposed rules. All those reasons I'd had the other night to push her away didn't seem so valid anymore.

The air between us grew thick, and I found myself leaning in. Her pupils widened at my close proximity.

"You need a bandage," she uttered.

"I'm fine," I whispered. But I wasn't. In fact, I was the furthest thing from it, and it didn't have a damn thing to do with the gash on my hand.

"Tucker." Her voice quaked, and she took half a step back. "I'm the nurse, and I say you need one, so go sit down." She pointed to the toilet seat.

Just this once, I decided to humor her. Slowly, I lowered the lid to keep it from slamming, and then I planted my ass on it. My eyes remained on Camryn, tracking her every movement.

She bent over to get something from under the sink, and my mind went to all the positions I wanted to take her in.

Camryn returned with the first aid kit, set it on the counter, and flipped the latch open. She withdrew a roll of gauze, medical tape, and butterfly strips. I intently watched her, enjoying the tender way she touched me, and I craved more.

When she finished, Camryn inspected her work. "There. You're good as new."

If only that were the case. I wanted her more than my next breath.

She took a step, but I reached out for her. Clasped the fingers of my injured hand over her wrist. The hold strained the adhesive strips beneath the bandage.

"Tucker," she whispered, "what are you doing?"

I stood and drew her body closer. Her perfect pink lips begged to be kissed. The hold on my self-control stretched taut. A small moan escaped her throat. That sexy fucking sound snapped the last bit of my restraint.

One arm went around Camryn's waist while my other hand went to the back of her head. My thumb skated over her jawline, down her neck, and back again.

"For days, all I've thought about is you." I trailed my thumb over her bottom lip. "Tasting you. Breathing in your scent. Fisting your gorgeous, dark hair in my fingers while I rained kisses against your skin." My thumb dipped under her chin, angled her face a fraction. I leaned in and scraped my soft beard on her cheek.

Voice low, I spoke against the shell of her ear, "If you

don't have any objections ... I'm going to kiss the hell out of you."

Her breath hitched, and I didn't have to wait long for her reply.

The single word came out as a plea. "Yes."

One hand rested at the base of her skull, her hair fisted in my other. My head dipped low to the curve where her neck and shoulder met, and my teeth nipped the sensitive skin. That one touch had Camryn's hands planted on either side of my rib cage. Slowly, I kissed my way toward her earlobe, captured it between my lips, and sucked.

"Tucker," she hissed. Slender fingers gripped my shirt. "Mmm."

My hand still planted on her waist journeyed upward. My lips moved over her jawbone to the corner of her mouth. I cupped her face between my palms, and my lips brushed against hers. Once. Then, twice. I tugged her bottom lip into my mouth and tilted her head just slightly.

Camryn pressed her body into me. My cock stiffened. God, I wanted her. My tongue darted out, seeking entrance, and when her lips parted, I delved inside. She tasted sweet, like vanilla and mint.

There was no fight for control. Camryn's body language spoke volumes ... she trusted me.

I kissed her long and deep until we were both breathless. Until the demand for oxygen could no longer be ignored. I wasn't ready to let her go. My hands stayed where they were, and I brought my forehead to hers.

We were panting breaths and racing hearts.

"Holy shit," she muttered.

Overtaken by the need to see her face, I took a step back and studied her. All glassy-eyed and dazed. "You okay?" I asked, amused.

"Don't move. Not yet." Her head dropped to my chest, and I wrapped my arms around her.

There wasn't any place else I wanted to be. Several long minutes passed before we left the bathroom.

Sweat beaded and then rolled down my back as I finished tightening up the alternator. Once the spark plugs, wires, and distributor cap were in place, I cleaned up the mess and put my tools away. Afterward, I went inside to inform Camryn I needed to take her car out for a test drive to make sure everything was in working order. Shayne was still asleep. Since I wasn't going far, I let her be.

About fifteen minutes later, I walked back into Camryn's house, keys in hand.

"You're all set," I said as I walked through the door.

Shayne and Camryn were sitting in the living room, surrounded by girlie shit.

"What do you want me to do with these?" The metal clanked together as I wiggled the key ring.

"Daddy," she squealed as she leaped up from her spot and barreled into me.

I lifted her into my arms for a hug.

Camryn held out her hand, so I set them in her palm and forced myself not to linger.

"Ew. Daddy, you're all sweaty." She held her nose. "And smelly, too," she added.

I set her on the floor and watched as she climbed back onto the couch.

"We have to do your other foot now," Shayne told her.

Camryn leaned back and placed her foot in Shayne's lap.

"Look," she said and held up her foot. "Camryn painted my toenails, and now, I get to paint hers."

She glanced at me and winked. "Thanks for taking care of Lucille."

I didn't miss the way she'd licked her lips. "You're welcome."

Shayne wasn't paying attention, but Camryn's eyes held mine. I rubbed my thumb across my bottom lip and gave her a wink. My reward was the smile she sent my way.

"Bug, we really need to go. I have to take a shower."

"Ah, but I'm not done." Shayne pushed out her lower lip.

My mouth opened to tell her she could finish later, but Camryn stopped me.

"We're having fun. Why don't you run home to shower, and she can stay here? Dinner should be ready when you get back."

"Please, Daddy. I promise I'll be good." She smiled the way she did when she wanted to get her way.

"You sure?" I asked Camryn. "I'll be back in fifteen minutes. Twenty, tops."

"Go. She'll be fine."

I nodded and strode out the door.

As I stood beneath the hot spray, my thoughts kept going back to Camryn and that kiss. She had been soft, pliable beneath my touch. I could easily become addicted to those lips. She was sexy, smart, funny, and a dozen other things I found attractive.

Seeing her with Bug today tugged at something in the deepest part of me. Camryn was so good with her. There didn't seem to be a selfish bone in her body. Some days, I wondered what it would be like to have the love of a woman who accepted the both of us. To wake up, wrapped in the arms of the same woman I'd sunk into the night before. And

I wanted to sink into Camryn. I wanted to fucking drown in her. Her scent. Her taste.

My dick was so hard, it was painful. I drew on the memory of the kiss and began to stroke myself. Fantasies of Camryn's body sprawled beneath me. Her lips around my dick. My head between her legs. I gripped tighter. My hand moved faster.

"Fuuuck," I roared and planted my injured hand on the ceramic to brace myself as the release took hold.

Hot cum shot onto the shower tiles as the climax tore through me, all the tension unraveled.

After finishing up in the shower, I tossed the wet bandage and dressed. My stomach growled, reminding me it'd been a long time since lunch, so I headed next door.

14

CAMRYN

A knock sounded on the front door, and since I was certain it was Tucker, I let Shayne answer it. Absently, I traced a finger over my lips. Hours later, that kiss still had me reeling.

"Hi, Daddy." Shayne's excited voice pulled me from my thoughts.

"Hey, Bug. Did you behave?" He bent to lift her into his arms.

"Of course."

"It smells good," Tucker said as he carried Shayne into the kitchen and sat her in the same barstool she'd used at lunch.

"Thanks. It'll be done in five."

"Can I do anything?"

"I've got it, but thanks for the offer. Help yourself to whatever you want to drink," I told him as I busied myself with removing the garlic bread from the oven.

He opened the fridge. "Do you want something?"

"Water is good."

Tucker grabbed three bottles and placed them at the bar.

I listened to Shayne tell him all about her day while I transferred the food to the island. Then, I grabbed plates, silverware, and salad bowls.

"I think that's everything. Anybody need anything else?" I asked.

"Can you grab me a knife, so I can cut up her spaghetti?"

"Sure," I said and walked to the drawer to get one out.

"Thank you."

I made my plate while Tucker made his and Shayne's. We sat in the same seats we'd been in at lunchtime.

I watched Tucker twirl the pasta around the tines of his fork and take a bite and swallow.

He turned his head toward me. "Camryn, this is amazing."

"It's so yummy," Shayne agreed.

"I'm glad you like it. There will be plenty left over. You guys can take some home." I bumped shoulders with Shayne. "So, did you have fun today?"

"Yes. A lot. I like you."

"You know what, kiddo? I like you, too."

I glanced over Shayne's head to find Tucker smiling at me.

Thank you, he mouthed.

You're welcome, I mouthed back.

We finished eating while Shayne's animated voice filled the silence. Tucker helped her down from her stool while I began to clear the dishes.

"I'll help you clean up," Tucker said.

"It's fine. I've got it."

"Yeah. Not happening. Why don't you go put on the TV for Shayne, and then we'll knock this out together?"

I stared at him, dumbfounded. "Where did you come from?"

"Camryn, I'm a grown-ass man. This is how it works."

"I don't think you understand." I walked over to him and crooked my finger for him to come closer. When he leaned down, I whispered in his ear, "A man who helps with dishes, it's so fucking hot. Like better than porn."

I left him to stare after me.

"Come on, sweet girl, let's find some cartoons." It was late, but I had cable. Surely, *Scooby-Doo* was on.

After I got her settled, I went back into the kitchen to help Tucker. I turned on the hot water and added a bit of dish soap for the stuff that couldn't go in the dishwasher.

Tucker came up behind me, one hand placed on either side, caging me in. "Better than porn, huh?" he spoke low against my ear. He ignored his cut, reached into the sudsy water, and covered my hands with his. "Should I assume your hands aren't the only things getting wet?" His lips faintly brushed my neck before he stepped back.

Holy shit.

"That wasn't nice."

"The flush on your cheeks says otherwise," he taunted.

I turned the faucet to cold, stuck my fingertips in the stream, and flicked water at him over my shoulder.

"Payback's a bitch." He chuckled.

I reached for a towel, pivoted, and stepped closer. "There," I said while I dried his face. "All better?"

He leaned back to glance into the living room to peek at Shayne. Then, he pulled me into the alcove just off the kitchen and backed me against the dryer. Tucker nipped my bottom lip and then tugged it between his. One hand snaked around my waist while the other tilted my head, angling my mouth just how he wanted it.

"You're like a fucking drug," he whispered against my mouth. His tongue dived inside.

Like a match to a fuse, the spark of desire grew to a blazing inferno.

My hands fisted his shirt, and I held on for dear life as he kissed me senseless.

"Tucker."

The sound of Shayne singing the *Scooby-Doo* theme song carried from the living room and broke through our sexual trance. We pulled away from each other, panting like we'd just run a marathon.

Tucker laughed and took a giant step back, almost looking sheepish. "We should finish up."

"Definitely."

We put away the food, and he rinsed the dishes while I loaded the dishwasher.

"Do you have plans next Saturday?" he asked while he rinsed the last plate.

"No. I don't think so. Why?"

"I want to take you out to dinner."

"Wait, so like a date?" I asked.

"Something like that."

"Sure." We were quiet for several beats, and then I added, "Thanks again ... for taking care of Lucille."

"You're welcome." He dried his hands on the dish towel. "We should probably get going."

I grabbed the container of still-warm spaghetti I'd packed for them and gave it to Tucker. "Here, don't forget this."

"I can't vouch for your car skills, but dinner was really good."

"Anyone ever tell you that you're a pain in the ass?" I teased.

"At least once a day." Together, we walked into the living room. "Bug, tell Camryn good night. It's bath time."

"Okay." She got up and walked over to where I stood.

I bent down, so I'd be at eye-level with her. Shayne's small arms wrapped around my neck as she tightly hugged me. I wanted to freeze this moment, so I could make it last a little longer. Shayne pulled back, and I reluctantly released her.

"Thank you for painting my nails and for the spaghetti," she told me.

"You're welcome, sweetheart." I stood, and Tucker reached for the door

He pulled it open, and Shayne bolted outside and across the lawn to their house. The motion detectors came on, illuminating the grass. Shayne danced in circles in the driveway.

"She's a great kid," I told him. "You've done an amazing job with her."

"Thanks." He reached into his back pocket and pulled out his phone. After he unlocked it, he gave it to me. "I need your number."

I took it from him, entered my contact information, and passed it back to him.

A light breeze sent a strand of my hair over my face. Tucker reached to brush it away, and the pad of his thumb skated across my cheek, sending a shiver down my spine.

He leaned into me. "Good night, Camryn," he whispered in my ear before he dropped his hand and walked away.

I closed the door and decided a bath sounded nice, so I went into the bathroom to fill the tub. I turned on the water and squirted bubble bath into the stream. While I waited, I stared at myself in the mirror, remembering earlier when Tucker's large frame had filled so much of the space.

Languidly, I traced a finger over my lips. I thought about the way his mouth had felt against mine.

Damn ... that man can kiss.

As soon as the thought entered my head, I started to wonder about all the other things he could do with that talented mouth of his. I shut the water off and slipped into the warmth. The light, airy sound of suds being disrupted echoed in my ears as I sank beneath them.

15

TUCKER

For the first time in years, I'd asked a woman to dinner.

Everything about Camryn drove me wild. Her laugh, how that tinkling sound built into something beautiful and unrestrained. Her quirky sense of humor. The blush that crept into her cheeks whenever she got embarrassed. The smell of her skin. I wanted to take her to bed and bury myself inside her for days. And I wanted more days like today.

A feeling both foreign yet familiar nagged at me. It took several seconds to place it. Happiness. That was what this was.

I crossed the lawn between Camryn's house and mine with a smile on my face. Shayne was waiting for me, twirling in the driveway without a care in the world.

"Did you have fun with Camryn today?" I asked as she stopped spinning and wobbled a bit. I reached out a hand to steady her.

"Yes. A lot." She giggled.

I opened the door and motioned for Shayne to go inside. "You really like her, don't you?"

"A whole bunch."

Me, too, kiddo.

I kept that thought to myself though.

"Daddy, can we watch a movie?"

"After bath time. Can you go put this in the fridge, please?" I passed Shayne the container of leftover spaghetti Camryn had sent home with us.

"Okay."

"I'm going to go start your bath."

"Can I have a fizzy bath?" she hollered as she skipped into the kitchen.

"Not tonight." It was the same answer I'd given her since I allowed it the first time.

I still felt like kicking myself in the ass for buying those damn things. Once you dropped the giant jawbreaker-looking object into the water, it would erupt like a little girl's dream and my worst nightmare.

Shayne had wanted a unicorn one because it turned the bath water different colors and spewed glitter every-fucking-where. So, I had given in, completely unaware of the havoc that thing would wreak. Nash had given me so much shit the next day at work because my forearms sparkled like I'd rolled them in diamond dust.

Yeah ... fizzy baths were strictly for Grammy's house.

I started the water and poured bubble bath into the stream. Bubbles I could handle. I grabbed a towel and went to the laundry to toss it into the dryer.

Already in the bathroom, Shayne had begun to strip out of her clothes when I walked back in. "Look at all those bubbles. Do I have time to play for a little while?"

"Yes, just try to keep the water in the tub tonight."

"Ah, man. I want to pretend I'm that guy from The Weather Channel." She carefully slipped into the water.

The kid was obsessed with storms and Jim Cantore.

"Negative, Bug. Hurricanes happen outside, not in the bathroom, and don't even think about starting the shower either."

"But I need rain for a hurricane."

"No hurricanes," I said, attempting a firm tone.

"Fine," she huffed. "But the last time wasn't my fault, Daddy."

"Is that right?" I asked, amused. "How did the bathroom get nearly flooded then?"

"My sandbags were useless against the storm surge."

That was because the "sandbags" had actually been washcloths she'd wrapped around her naked Barbies, which she lined up on the edge of the tub. Not only had the floor gotten soaked, but she'd also cleaned out every washcloth from the damn towel closet.

I had no idea how she came up with this shit.

"You make me crazy, you know that?"

"Yep. But you love me." She batted her eyes and smiled wide.

"I do. But I mean it ... no pretending to be a force of nature. I'll be back in a few minutes."

She was old enough to wash herself, but her hair was long, and she still needed help.

"Maybe I'll pretend to be a sea creature."

I shook my head as I walked out of the bathroom, knowing full well I'd end up mopping the floor. After I changed clothes, I went back to check on her. I stood just outside the doorway for a minute, listening to her play. Despite everything, the kid thrived. She was smart and funny, and she had the purest heart.

"Ready to wash your hair, Bug?" I asked gently. She hadn't seen me, and I didn't want to scare her.

"In a second. Come watch me play." She pointed to the toilet.

I dropped the lid and took a seat, bracing my elbows on my knees.

"Do I have school tomorrow?"

"No. Tomorrow is Sunday."

"We're going to Grammy's for Sunday supper, right?"

"Yes."

"Daddy, do you think Camryn can come to supper at Grammy's?"

"I'm sure she's busy."

"But maybe we could ask her to come sometime. I like her. She plays with me, and she's really nice. And pretty. Don't you think she's pretty?"

Pretty was too plain a word for Camryn. Beautiful, exquisite, gorgeous. Those were much more fitting.

"Yes, I think she's pretty."

"Her mommy left, too."

The comment took me by surprise.

"Shayne, your mommy didn't leave you, baby. She died."

"Yes, but she still left." She didn't look at me. Instead, she swam her naked Barbie through the water. "Camryn's mommy didn't die, but she left. She didn't want to be her mommy anymore. Isn't that so sad?"

"It is sad." I wanted to know where all this was coming from. "Bug, did Camryn ask you about your mom?"

Camryn didn't strike me as the type of person who would pump Shayne for information, but I had to ask.

"Nope." She looked thoughtful. "I asked her if her mommy painted her nails when she was a little girl like me, and she said she didn't have a mommy. I told her that is just silly because everybody has a mommy. But she said her mommy didn't want to be a mommy anymore so she left," she said matter-of-fact. Then, she gathered bubbles into her palm, tipped her head back, and spread the suds over her jaw and under her nose. "Look, I have a beard, just like you."

I didn't know what to make of Shayne's news, but now wasn't the time to dwell on it.

"You're so silly." I scooped up some bubbles and then blew them out of my open hand, making it rain soapsuds.

"Daddy." She giggled.

"Time to wash your hair."

She laid her head back into the water to wet the top while I grabbed the baby shampoo from the shelf. After squirting some into my hand, I knelt on the floor, and Shayne sat crisscross in the water with her back toward me.

She tilted her head back, hazel irises meeting mine. "Don't get it in my eyes," she reminded me.

"I won't."

"But, sometimes, you do."

"I'll be extra careful."

Her lips pursed together as she considered my promise, and then she leaned forward. I gathered her wet hair and worked it into a lather. Afterward, I used a cup to rinse out the soap. My knees popped as I stood.

"What was that?"

"Just the sound of your daddy getting old."

"You're not old. Wait. How old are you?"

"Thirty."

"That is only a little bit old." She held her thumb and index finger about an inch apart. "I can count to one hundred fifty. Thirty comes near the beginning, so that makes you only a teeny pinch old."

"I like your logic, kid. I'll be right back. I'm going to get your towel from the dryer."

"Hurry or else I will be cold," she called after me.

Shayne stood with her arms in the air as soon as I stepped back into the bathroom.

"Press the stopper, Bug."

She bent over to press the knob. Seconds later, water gurgled down the drain. Shayne thrust her arms back in the air, and I wrapped her in the warm, oversized cotton.

"It's so toasty," she said, snuggling into my neck.

"You're so spoiled."

"And you're the best daddy in the whole wide world."

I grabbed the brush from the counter, carried her into her room, and sat down on her bed with her in my lap. She nestled into me and let out a yawn.

"Sleepy?"

"Nope."

Of course she wouldn't admit it.

I squeezed the excess water from her hair and ran the brush through it. "All right, kiddo, time to get into your jammies."

She hugged the towel to her and shoved off my lap.

I left her to it and went into the kitchen. It was an ice cream kind of night, so I reached into the freezer and pulled out the chocolate. Since the container was close enough to empty, I decided to forgo the bowl and grabbed two spoons from the silverware drawer. Then, I went to the living room.

Just as I turned on the television, Shayne came into the room, dragging her quilt in one hand and Wilbur clutched in the other. I set the ice cream carton on the end table and sat in the recliner.

"Did you remember to hang your towel up?"

"Oops. Hold this." She gave me her blanket. "I'll be right back." Her small, bare feet smacked against the floor as she ran.

When she returned, I lifted her into my lap, arranging the blanket around us. "What do you want to watch, baby?"

"*Beauty and the Beast.*"

I flipped through the DVR, pushed play, and reached for the ice cream, passing a spoon to Shayne. Contentedly, we ate our dessert and watched the movie. After we finished, I set the box back on the table and raised the leg rest on the chair.

Shayne was engrossed in the television, her plush pig clenched to her chest. I pressed my lips to the crown of her head and inhaled her clean baby scent.

"Love you, Bug," I whispered into her still-damp hair.

"Love you, Daddy," she whispered back. Her head rested against my chest, and within a few minutes, she was fast asleep.

I thought back to what Shayne had said earlier. Judging Camryn's mom would make me a hypocrite. Even though I couldn't imagine life without my daughter, there had been a time when this was the last thing I ever wanted.

I held Shayne for a long time. Just to listen to her breathe. Life moved so damn fast, and I knew moments like this would become fewer.

When the movie was over, I carried my sleeping girl to her bed, tucked her in, and quietly kissed her good night.

I went into the kitchen, and just like always, the first thing my eyes settled on was the photograph on the fridge of the three of us together. There were pictures of Dani scattered throughout the house. Some of the three of us together while others were of Shayne and her mom.

But this one ...

I couldn't help but look at it several times a day.

The one that picked at the scars and never let them completely mend.

The one that served as a constant, tangible reminder.

Whenever I looked at it, I smelled the nauseating combination of cafeteria food and antiseptic. I heard the beeping monitors and background noise. I saw the panic, devastation, and longing in her eyes. I felt her life sift through my fingers like grains of sand. I tasted the saltiness of our tears as we tried like hell to console each other.

A snapshot of the past that made it hard to breathe in the present. And I wanted to fucking breathe.

I pressed my forehead to the cool metal surface. One hand went to the magnet while the other went to the corner of the photograph. I lifted my head and slid the magnet away, gripping the picture between my thumb and forefinger, and then I lowered myself onto one of the chairs and stared at the image.

After several long minutes, I stood from the chair and strode into my bedroom, closing the door behind me. My bare feet sank into the carpet as I crossed the room and discarded the picture on the mattress. Then, I made my way over to the small walk-in closet. I already felt it—the pain that I knew would hurt like hell. Acid dripped into a wound that had yet to fully heal. I stretched my arms over my head to grasp a box on the top shelf.

Grief gripped my insides as I carried it to the bed, sat, and removed the lid. Dani's delicate handwriting stared back at me.

THE RULES …

MAKE HER FEEL LOVED EVERY SINGLE DAY.

RAISE HER TO BE A GOOD HUMAN.

DON'T LET HER GROW UP TO BE AN ENTITLED BRAT.

READ HER BEDTIME STORIES AND TEACH HER THE BIG WORDS.

REMIND HER THAT EVERYBODY FALLS; IT'S HOW YOU RISE THAT
MATTERS.
LET HER BE HER OWN PERSON.
BELIEVE IN HER, ESPECIALLY WHEN SHE DOESN'T BELIEVE IN
HERSELF.
PUSH HER OUT OF HER COMFORT ZONE A LITTLE, SO SHE'LL LEARN
TO EMBRACE LIFE.
TELL HER HOW MUCH I LOVED HER.
AS FOR YOU, TUCKER ... LIVE WELL. LIVE FOR THOSE OF US WHO
DON'T HAVE THE CHANCE.

One more rule had been scrawled at the bottom. My eyes purposely shifted from it without bothering to read the words. I knew what it said, and it was her one request I wasn't sure I could grant.

The words floated on the page. My eyes shifted to the contents of the open box. On top lay a picture of the six of us —Griffin, Holly, Nash, Macy, Dani, and me. The snapshot had been taken when we were in high school, during a beach bonfire. It was a lifetime ago, but I remembered it well. I smiled despite the way my chest constricted. Setting aside the paper, I reached inside for the photo. We were young and ignorant to how cruel the world could be. Back then ... life had been full of possibilities. Never in a million years had I thought it would play out like this.

I picked up the image of me, Dani, and Shayne and held it next to the one of the six of us. Side by side, I stared at the faces frozen in time. Nobody would classify what I'd done over the last four years as living. One day had faded into the next while I just tried to make it through. I took care of my daughter, looked after my mom, and kept the business running. I existed and did what needed to be done, but it wasn't living. Not really.

Live.

The word clanked inside my head. Pinged and rico-cheted like the ball from an old arcade game.

Live.

I felt it take root.

Live.

I put the contents back in the box, added the photo from the fridge, secured the lid, and returned it to the closet. Then, I went in search of my phone. There it was, sitting on top of the dresser, where I'd left it before I gave Shayne a bath. I opened the screen and searched my Contacts for Camryn's name.

Live.

Me: So, next Saturday ...

I didn't expect her to text back. Despite the late hour, the little dots jumped on the screen.

Camryn: Tucker?
Me: Who did you think it was?
Camryn: Are you having second thoughts?
Me: Definitely not.
Camryn: So, like a date?
Me: No. Not like a date. It is a date.
Camryn: Are you still going to feed me?

Her response brought a smile to my face.

Me: Yes.
Camryn: Do I need to dress up?
Me: That's up to you.
Camryn: Can I wear yoga pants?

The question conjured up an image of her perfect ass. My dick twitched. We'd never make it to dinner.

Me: Not a chance.
Camryn: So ... it really is a date.
Me: Yes.

16

CAMRYN

I'd been looking forward to my date with Tucker all week long, and by the time Saturday rolled around, my nerves had started to get the best of me. Tucker would be here in less than thirty minutes, and it wasn't like he had far to walk. Hopefully, he wasn't one of those people who arrived fifteen minutes early for everything. People like that made me crazy. Mainly because I wanted to be one of them. Of the character traits I possessed, timeliness didn't make the list. I could leave the house an hour before necessary and still be five minutes late.

The metal plates of the straightener clamped together as I positioned the iron over the last section of my hair. Slowly, I glided it down the length of my hair. Mouth twisted, I took in my long raven locks, toying with which side to let it fall on, the silky warm strands cascading between my fingers. Happy with the way it looked, I shut off the iron and started working on my makeup.

I considered myself a minimalist when it came to beauty products. My face was bare unless I was working, and on those days, I wore mascara, a little bit of blush, and lip gloss.

Tonight though ... I wanted to look sexy. I took my time with applying eyeliner, shadow, and lip liner in addition to what I normally wore to work.

Finished, I stepped back and studied my reflection in the full-length mirror on the back of the bathroom door.

I wore a white cami underneath a cobalt-blue sheer blouse, paired with black skinny jeans and black peep-toe flats. This particular shade of blue made my eyes pop, and the eyeliner made it even more dramatic.

Just as I finished finger-combing through my hair one last time, a loud knock sounded from the living room. My heart rate accelerated. I'd had butterflies before, but these weren't butterflies as much as a flock of pterodactyls ready to take flight in my stomach.

Twack. Twack. Twack. The thuds came in quick succession.

"Coming," I called out and headed toward the door. "It's just Tucker," I reminded myself.

He'd pretty much seen me at my worst already, given our initial encounter and the night I cried in his arms. After that, I had nowhere to go but up. My fingers twisted the knob, and I drew in a calming breath before opening it.

Tucker stood on my porch, dressed in a black button-down shirt that looked custom made for his body. Clad in a pair of well-worn jeans distressed to perfection. Beard neatly trimmed. Sexy smirk in place.

"Hi," I said.

"Hi." Hazel irises roamed over my body before they made a slow return to my face. "Damn. You look beautiful."

He leaned down to plant a kiss on my cheek. Rough whiskers grazed my skin, causing the blood to hum in my veins. A hint of spice, citrus, and cedar filled my nose. The scent uniquely Tucker.

"You look nice, too." Nice didn't even begin to cover it. He was the sexiest man I'd ever laid eyes on.

"Ready to go?" he asked.

"Just let me grab my purse." I ambled to the makeshift coffee table, picked it up, and locked the door on my way out.

Tucker led the way to his truck and opened my door. He waited for me to climb in before he shut it and went around to the other side.

As we backed out of the driveway, I turned to him. "Is Shayne at your mom's?"

"Yeah. Mom keeps her overnight once or twice a month."

"That's nice. I'm sure it's not easy, doing it all on your own."

Tucker glanced at me with an expression I couldn't read before shifting his eyes back to the road.

"When I was growing up, it was just me and my dad," I explained. "Shayne and I have that in common."

Tucker nodded in understanding. "It is hard. I'm not going to pretend it isn't."

"Well ... for what it's worth, I think you're doing a phenomenal job."

"I appreciate that." After a beat, he asked, "Are you still close to your dad?"

I stared out the window, trying to keep my emotions in check. "We used to be ... he passed six months ago."

"I'm sorry." His hand closed the space between us, reaching for mine. He lightly squeezed it before placing his back on the wheel.

"It's crazy. I still pick up the phone to call him, and midway through dialing his number, I remember he's not here. I'm a grown woman, but sometimes, I'm still that little girl who misses her dad." I blinked back the unshed tears. "I'm so sorry. This isn't really first-date conversation."

"Camryn, there aren't any rules. It's just you and me."

"Tell me about your family," I prodded him, ready to have the attention off me.

"There isn't much to tell. Most of my extended family have either passed or moved away from here. It's just me, Mom, and Bug." A shadow crossed his face and then disappeared just as fast. "Nash and Macy are family, but we're not actually related."

"Wait. Macy? Does she work at Jaxson Realty?"

"Yep." He smirked.

"When Shayne mentioned an Aunt Macy, I didn't realize it was one in the same."

"We grew up together."

"It really is a small world."

"Tell me about your mom," Tucker said.

I had no way of knowing if Shayne had brought up our conversation, so I decided to lay it out. "The other day, while you worked on the car, Shayne asked me about her. When I said I didn't have a mom, it sort of led down a winding road."

"She mentioned that your mom left. What happened?"

My eyes shifted out the window.

"You don't have to answer if you don't want to."

"The topic of my mom is kind of a sore spot." I'd had years to accept the fact that she didn't love us enough to stick around. As I'd gotten older, I understood her actions reflected her character, not mine. Regardless, as much as I liked to pretend it didn't bother me, the effects of her abandonment were long reaching. I cleared my throat. "She left when I was three. Decided that family life wasn't for her and took off. I haven't seen her since."

"I'm sorry ..."

"Don't be. It's life. You don't get to choose your hand, but you can decide how to play the cards."

"You're pretty amazing, you know that." It was a statement not a question.

I shook my head. "Not really. Dwelling on it won't change the situation. Hating her would give her power."

"If I can do half the job with Bug that your dad did with you, I'll have raised one hell of a kid."

"I think that is one of the best compliments I've ever been given, thank you. And, for the record, you already are."

We'd been driving for about twenty minutes when Tucker pulled into the parking lot of a restaurant.

"Don't move," he ordered as he shut off the truck and got out. His gentlemanly ways were sexy as hell.

I waited for him to come around to open my door. When he did, he offered me his hand. Once I was safely on the ground, he gently tugged me closer, dipped his head low, and tenderly brushed his lips over mine. Then, Tucker reached into the truck to get my purse off the seat, gave it to me, and shut the door.

"Thank you," I said as I fell into step beside him.

He placed his palm on the small of my back and guided me through the open door to the host stand.

"Welcome to Driftwood Landing," a young man greeted us.

"Reservation for Jaxson," Tucker informed him.

"Of course, sir."

The podium had a built-in screen, and the host's eyes sifted through the list. After he located the reservation, he gestured to the girl standing beside him. Her smile was friendly.

"Brittany will show you to your table."

"Right this way," she said.

The heat from his hand radiated through mine as we followed behind her through the restaurant to an outdoor deck. Tucker pulled out my chair, and waited until I sat, before taking his seat. He was charming, considerate, and sweet. I bit my lip to keep from laughing at the thought.

Sweet.

Six foot three, all broad shoulders, calloused hands, and chiseled man from head to toe. Sweet certainly wasn't the most suitable adjective for a man like Tucker Jaxson.

"May I get you something to drink while you wait?" Brittany asked as she placed a menu in front of each of us.

"Yes, please. I'll have water with lime," I said.

"And for you, sir?"

"Sam Adams, please."

"I'll be right back with those."

Our table overlooked the water, offering a spectacular view of the sun that had just begun to set. Shades of pink and orange swept brilliantly across the sky, making it seem more like a painting than real life.

Salty sea air filled my lungs as I drew in a breath and then released it on a sigh. "This view is absolutely breathtaking."

"It certainly is."

I glanced at Tucker, but his eyes weren't taking in our surroundings. He was staring at me.

"You really do look beautiful," he complimented.

"Thank you," I said shyly.

The intensity of his gaze ignited a warmth between my legs.

"Pardon me for the intrusion," a woman said as she set our drinks on the table. "I'm Marisol, and I'll be taking care of you this evening." Her smile was warm and friendly.

"Have you had a chance to look at the menu, or do you need a few minutes?" she asked, her finger pushing the glasses higher on her nose.

"Good evening." Tucker smiled at her and then added, "We'd like a few minutes if you don't mind."

"Of course. I'll be back to check on you shortly."

He opened his menu, and I followed suit.

"Since I've never been here, what's good?"

"Do you like seafood? The sea scallops are really good."

"That sounds amazing." I closed my menu and placed it back on the table.

A few minutes later, Marisol returned with a small basket of artisan bread and two small plates. Since we were ready, she took our order.

After she left, I studied Tucker. "Can I ask you something?"

"Sure."

"Will you tell me about Shayne's mom?"

He stared out at the horizon for so long, I wasn't sure he'd answer.

"Her name was Dani. We got married when she was eight months pregnant with Shayne."

"How long has she been ..." The words hung in the air as my voice trailed off.

"She died when Bug was a little over a year old."

The look on his face made me wish I hadn't asked.

"Tucker, I'm so sorry."

"It's okay. It was a long time ago."

"How did you meet?"

He picked up his beer, sat back in his chair, and lifted the bottle to his lips, taking a long pull before answering, "I'd known her practically my whole life. She moved to Jaxson Cove when she was seven to live with her grandparents. Her mom and dad had been killed in a plane crash."

"Oh my God. That's horrible."

"It was. She had a rough go of it for a long time."

I reached for a piece of bread. "So, were you two, like, high school sweethearts?"

A strange look crossed his face. Slightly amused and a little bit wistful. "No, actually, we weren't." His eyes met mine, and he opened his mouth but closed it again when Marisol returned with our entrees.

"Who gets the sea scallops?"

Tucker pointed to me.

"Be careful; the plate is warm," she warned as she set it in front of me. "This must be yours." She smiled and placed the other plate in front of Tucker.

He'd opted for the New York strip steak.

"Everything look okay?"

"Yes, thank you," Tucker replied.

"Let me know if y'all need anything else."

I watched as Tucker cut into his steak. Then, he speared it on his fork before he lifted it to his lips and put it in his mouth. I wanted to feel those lips on mine again.

"Camryn?"

"Mmhmm?" My tongue swiped across my bottom lip.

"Camryn."

My face flushed with heat. I took a drink of my water, suddenly wishing I'd ordered something stronger. "Yes?"

"You should eat before it gets cold," he said with a smirk.

"Right." I picked up my fork, cut a scallop in half, stuck it in my mouth, and attempted to cover my embarrassment.

17

TUCKER

Between the setting sun and the clear lights strung around the deck, I was able to see the flush of Camryn's cheeks. She was so fucking adorable.

"Do you want a bite?" I gestured toward my plate.

"Sharing food ... isn't that more like a second-date sort of thing?"

"Already trying to get me to go out with you again?" I chuckled.

She pointed her fork at me. "You should really work on your self-esteem."

She laughed a full belly laugh, and I knew I was screwed. When it came to this woman, I was so fucking screwed.

She stole a piece of steak from my plate, and since I wasn't about to let her get one over on me, I stabbed one of her scallops and popped it into my mouth.

The conversation was light and easy as we finished our meal. We ordered a slice of key lime pie to share for dessert. After the check was paid and I left a generous tip, we took the steps that led from the deck down onto the beach.

Camryn slipped out of her shoes and carried them in her hand.

We walked along the shoreline for a few minutes before I broke the silence. "Tell me about Jared."

"There isn't much to say." She stared down the beach and then at her feet. "He's an asshole. End of story."

"Tell me what happened between you two. Is there a chance you will work it out?"

Granted, that last question might make me sound like a pussy, but I needed to know. Shayne was growing more attached to her as time went on. Truth be told, I was too.

"Work it out?" She nearly choked on the words. "Oh, I assure you, Tucker, there is no way that will happen."

"Tell me."

She let out an exasperated huff. "Jared and I met when he came into the urgent care center where I used to work. We dated for about a year, and then he proposed. We were engaged for about two months when my dad died." Her voice cracked at the mention of her father. "Losing him was a shock. He was the picture of health, and then one day, he had a massive heart attack. I was such a mess. Instead of Jared being there for me, he was there for his administrative assistant. One day, I walked into the apartment Jared and I shared to find them fucking on my couch."

Both fists clenched at my sides. Fucker had better not even think about showing his face here. "Is that piece of shit the reason you moved?"

"Partly. I had no desire to keep my dad's house. It wasn't home, and I didn't have any ties to Booker Ridge other than my job. My dad had moved there for work when I left for college, and I'd wanted to be close to him when I graduated. With him gone, there was no reason to stay."

Waves rolled onto the shore, and an easy silence fell

between us. We had wandered a distance from the restaurant, so I lightly gripped Camryn's arm to turn us around. Her orange blossom and honey scent wafted on the breeze and made a beeline straight to my dick. I couldn't wait another second to claim her lips. I draped an arm around her waist and pulled her close. My hands moved to Camryn's face, cupping her cheeks in my palms.

"You're so fucking beautiful," I whispered against her mouth.

Gently, my lips brushed hers. Then, I trailed my tongue across her bottom lip, urging her to part for me. When she did, I slipped inside. She tasted so fucking good. Sweet with just a hint of lime that lingered from our dessert.

Her hands held on to my waist as I took the kiss deeper. She moaned into my mouth, and I swallowed her sound. I wanted more. Needed more. One of my hands shifted to the back of her head, lost in the silky black strands of her hair. I kissed her long and deep until she pressed lightly against me, desperate to drag air into her lungs.

Camryn's head rested in the middle of my chest as she tried to catch her breath. "Holy shit." Her words were muffled into my skin.

I chuckled softly. "You know, that's what you said the last time I kissed you."

"That was ... I mean ... wow."

Thankful for the darkness that hid my stiff cock, I took her by the hand, and we continued walking back to the truck. When we got home, I parked in my driveway and walked Camryn to her door.

"Do you want to come inside for a drink?"

"All right." I took the keys from her.

We went inside, and I followed her into the kitchen. Camryn took two bottles of beer from the fridge and passed me one. We both twisted off our caps and took a drink at the same time. She propped herself against the island while I leaned on the opposite counter, facing her. It had been years since I wanted a woman like I wanted her. She was a magnet, and the closer I got, the harder I tried to resist the attraction, the greater the pull. From the way she'd kissed me back on the beach, I knew she felt it, too.

She lifted the bottle back to her mouth. My dick had been semi-hard since we left the beach, and it grew harder as I watched those sexy, sinful lips part over the glass rim. Her pink tongue darted out to lick her bottom lip.

Camryn's eyes never left mine as I closed the distance between us. I set my bottle on the counter, took hers out of her grasp, and placed it alongside mine. My hands found her waist. I lifted her onto the island and stood between her open legs. My thumb brushed the shell of her ear as I tucked her hair behind it. I kissed the sensitive spot just behind her earlobe.

"Oh God, Tucker."

Fuck ... I loved the way she purred my name.

Moving lower, I nipped lightly at her neck. "What are you doing to me, woman?" I whispered against her skin.

"Tucker, please."

"Please what, darlin'?"

"Kiss me."

My lips trailed upward, over her neck and across her jawbone, before I finally settled on her mouth. Her lips parted, and I slipped my tongue between them. Our movements became frenzied. Insane with need and desperate for more, I carried her to the couch, never breaking the seal of our kiss.

She straddled my lap. "Tucker," she moaned my name.

My hands went to her ass as she rocked against me. I

wanted to be inside her so fucking bad. It wouldn't be a one-time thing. With Camryn, it wouldn't be just sex, and I knew that. It would mean something. Two seconds away from stripping her bare, I knew I had to slow down, no matter how much my dick protested.

I pulled away. Camryn's chest heaved while she tried to catch her breath. Her perfect tits were right there in my face. I fought the urge to slide my hand beneath her shirt, cup her breast, and tease her nipple. I summoned every ounce of willpower I had as I placed my hands on her hips to still her movements and forced my eyes to her face.

"Camryn, look at me."

When she met my gaze, the same desire and longing I felt was reflected back at me.

"I should probably go."

She meant something to me, and I was determined not to fuck it up.

Rejection filled her blue eyes. Resolve washed over her features as she got off my lap and stood. "You're right. It's late," she said, arms crossed over her chest, her eyes looking anywhere but at me.

I rose from the couch and reached for her, but she took a step back.

"Don't do that."

"Do what?" she asked defiantly. Her refusal to look at me told me everything I needed to know. "It's fine. I get it."

"No, you don't." Gently, I gripped her chin between my thumb and index finger and forced her to meet my eyes. "Don't pull away from me." I snaked an arm around her waist and moved my hand from her chin to the back of her head. Splaying my fingers, I skated my thumb across her cheek. "Camryn, as much as I want you ..." I leaned my fore-head to hers. "And I do fucking want you," I confessed and then drew back, so I could look at her. "Whatever is happening between us, I don't want to screw it up. Walking out that door is the last thing I want to do. If I stay, I won't be able to be here and not touch you."

She placed her hands on my chest. "What if I want you to touch me?"

"What if I want more?" I grazed my lips softly against hers one more time. "Good night, Camryn."

I released her and headed for the door but then turned back. I kissed her one more time, unhurried, and this time, she was the one to pull away.

"Night, Tucker."

"Lock up behind me."

"I will."

I twisted the knob, stepped onto the porch, and shut the door behind me. Once the lock clicked into place, I started for home, and it was the last fucking thing I wanted to do.

18

CAMRYN

I stood in my living room for several long minutes. Finger to my swollen lips. I'd never been kissed the way Tucker had kissed me tonight. Desire radiated in my core with a need so strong, it tempted me to open the door and go after him. Without warning, I heard the sky burst into a downpour, effectively detouring the notion.

Resigned, I forced my feet to move across the hardwood floor into the kitchen. I opened the cabinet for a wineglass and then reached for the uncorked bottle of green apple Riesling in the fridge. Just as I filled the tumbler, a knock came from the front door.

The sound tugged me from my lust-induced haze. Wine abandoned on the counter, I made my way through the living room. There was only one person it could be. Still, I looked through the peephole anyway. Tucker was standing on the front porch, shirt untucked, hair mussed, soaked to the bone.

I opened the door. "Tucker?"

Moonlight spilled behind him, acting as a backlight to his well-built frame. "Ask me to stay."

My brows furrowed in confusion. "What?"

He ran a hand through his hair, sloughing off some of the water. "Ask me to stay," he repeated.

"I never wanted you to go." My fingers fisted his drenched shirt, pulling him through the entryway.

He kicked the door shut, rotated our bodies, clasped my wrists, and pinned my arms against the door. He sucked my bottom lip between his teeth.

"Ah," I moaned.

That one little sound had him swirling his tongue against mine. I felt the wetness between my legs. Every pass of his lips made me wetter. When he broke the kiss, I whimpered at the loss.

Hard, panted breaths coasted across my skin. "I need to be inside you, baby. If you aren't ready, you need to tell me now."

"Tucker, I want you. Please."

"You have on too many fucking clothes," he growled.

The grip on my wrists fell away. Layer by layer, he peeled me out of my clothes until I stood before him in nothing but a white lace bra and matching thong. His eyes raked over my body.

"Fucking stunning. Are you wet for me?" His gravelly voice scraped my flesh while one hand began a slow descent down my body.

Holy shit.

If it were possible to come from words alone, I'd have splintered apart.

I pressed my body into him, and my fingers went to the buttons of his shirt. Unfastening them one by one.

Lust-drunk and brave, I lifted my eyes to his. "Maybe."

He shifted the sheer material out of the way, dipped his finger inside me, and circled my clit with his thumb. "You're drenched." Tucker slowly kissed me, the glide of his tongue matching the slide of his finger. "Do you like that, baby?"

Answering the question with my body, I bucked into his palm, frantic for more. He added another finger and pumped faster, fucking my pussy the same way he was fucking my mouth.

"Tucker—*ah*." I was close.

When he withdrew his fingers, I let out a frustrated groan.

"We have all night, baby. The first time you come will be on my tongue." He sucked his thumb clean.

Never in my life had I'd been so turned on.

He picked me up, and my legs curled around his waist. "Bedroom. Now."

"Down the hall. Second door on the left."

19

TUCKER

My fingers dug into Camryn's ass as I carried her down the hall. I wanted to bury myself between her legs for days. Knowing how sweet she tasted, I needed more than the little sample I'd had. With the door already open, I walked toward the bed and gently deposited her onto the mattress. Finishing the job she'd started, I took off my clothes and dropped them on the floor.

"Do you know how much I want you?" I asked, pulling her to her feet.

Then, I captured her mouth in a soft kiss while I unfastened her bra and slid it down her arms to join the pile. My cock twitched against her belly.

"Tucker, please. Hurry."

I loved the sound of my name on her lips, and I intended to make her scream it. She leaned against my shoulder, neck exposed, begging to be kissed. I bit into the sensitive flesh, cupped her tits, and rolled her pebbled nipples between my fingers.

"Tucker, oh God." Her nails dug into my wrists.

"You like that, don't you?"

"Yes."

I stepped back and slipped the last barrier between us to the floor. A hunger like I'd never known rumbled through me. The light from the moon shone through the blinds, allowing me to see her gorgeous body. Perfect tits, toned arms, soft curves, lean legs. She was better than any image I'd created in my head.

"Do you have any idea how fucking stunning you are?"

She grazed her nails over my chest and down my stomach. "Show me."

Her hands moved lower, but I caught them.

"Come sit." I led her over to the edge of the bed, and when she sat, I dropped to my knees. "I've thought about this for days ... how you would taste. What it would feel like when I buried myself inside you."

I gripped Camryn's ankles and spread her wide. Lowering my head between her legs, I licked up her wet center, gently sucking her clit between my lips. Working her over with my tongue. Sliding it back all the way down before I dipped inside her and then repeating it. As I tightened my grip on her legs, the tip of my tongue flicked over the sensitive bud. I couldn't get enough of her.

Her hands fisted my hair. "Tucker—*ahhh*." Her hips bucked against my mouth. "I'm close. So fucking close. Please don't stop." Her legs quaked as the tremor started to roll through her. "*Ahhh*." She came hard, her taste coating my tongue. As she came down from her orgasm, a smile spread over her face. "Th-that. Was fuck-ing. A-mazing," she panted.

I claimed her mouth in a kiss. Knowing she tasted herself was erotic.

"We're just getting started, baby." Reaching for my jeans,

I grabbed the condoms from the back pocket and tossed them onto the mattress.

Camryn moved to the head of the bed and lay back on the pillows. I'd seen some beautiful things in my life, but everything paled in comparison to her. Her long black hair was fanned out around her, a stark contrast against the white pillows. Her lips, I never wanted to stop kissing them, and pebbled dusty-pink nipples were begging for my mouth. I loved the curve of her hips and how there was a softness about her. I wanted to worship every inch of her.

Starting at her ankles, I worked my way up her body, planting kisses along the way. "Your body was made for me," I said when I made it to her lips.

Her tongue swirled with mine, and she lifted her hips, grinding her wetness on my cock.

"So eager." I chuckled against her mouth. I dipped my head to her tits and sucked a hard nipple between my teeth.

"Mmm," she moaned.

My hand glided down her body to her clit. I rubbed slow circles on her bundle of nerves.

"Oh God." She bucked against my hand.

"I need to be inside you, baby."

"Hurry."

I located the condom, sheathed my cock, and gradually slid inside her. Stretching her walls around me, I pushed in until I was fully seated. I started to move, slowly dragging my shaft in and out, desperate to make it last as long as possible. Picking up the pace, I thrust deeper.

Camryn dug her nails into my back.

Stinging pain and pleasure mixed together, driving me to the edge. "You feel so fucking good, baby."

"Tucker. More. Please," she begged.

Need surged through me. Unable to hold back, I pounded into her. Faster, harder.

"Oh *Gooood*, Tucker."

She screamed my name as she tipped over the edge, and I followed right behind her, our sounds joining forces. As we both cried out our release, I held on to her and then continued long after because I didn't want to let her go.

20

CAMRYN

Curled into Tucker's arms and sated from the best sex I'd ever had in my life, I was ready to sleep, but my bladder had other ideas. "I'll be right back. I have to go to the bathroom."

Tucker stretched his arms above his head. "I'm going to grab a bottle of water. Do you want one?"

"Sure."

Inside the bathroom, I caught sight of myself in the mirror. Messy hair, raccoon eyes, and a ridiculous smile I felt all the way to my toes. After I took care of business, I washed my face and ran a brush through my hair. There was no hope for that stupid smile though.

Tucker still wasn't in bed when I got back. His discarded clothes lay strewed on the floor, so I picked them up. I folded his jeans and placed them on the dresser. My hands lingered on his shirt, and I brought it up to my nose. Soft, slightly damp, his scent interwoven into the fabric.

"Mmm."

"That good, huh?"

I jumped, dropping the shirt to the floor. "You scared me to death."

He laughed hard. Really hard. "I'm sorry," he finally got out. "Why are you sniffing my shirt?"

"If you must know, I like the way you smell." I bent to pick it up and placed it on top of his jeans. "Also, what is it with you and scaring the shit outta me?" Hands on my hips, I attempted a glare. Since I was naked and still smiling, it wasn't very unconvincing.

"I'm sorry." He opened the other bottle of water in his hand and gave it to me.

"Sure you are." I poked him in the chest as I walked by and lifted the water to my lips, taking a drink before placing it on the nightstand.

Tucker pulled the bedding back, and we climbed in and rolled to our sides, facing each other. He pushed the hair off my forehead and stared at me. Hazel eyes fixed on my blue ones.

"You scare the shit out of me, too."

"You have nothing to worry about. I'm harmless, and in all fairness, sniffing your clothing doesn't make me a stage-five clinger," I joked.

Only Tucker didn't smile, and I knew we weren't talking about the shirt anymore.

He reached for my hand and laced our fingers together. "At the risk of sounding like a pussy"—he kissed the back of my hand—"baby, you fucking terrify me."

That was the last thing I'd expected him to say. The confession dug into my flesh and marred my heart. "Why?"

"Because you make me want things that I don't know how to have. Sex is one thing; a relationship is another."

He'd been a widower for over four years.

"You haven't had a relationship since … how is that even possible?" I raised a brow at him.

The strangest look passed over his face. "It's not what you think. Sex is a lot less complicated, and I come with a lot of baggage."

"Shayne isn't baggage." I hated the context of the word. I'd been someone's baggage.

"You know what I mean, and honestly, it's a lot to ask of someone, but I've never met anyone who made me want more."

"Is that what you want? A relationship, I mean." I held my breath, unsure of what I wanted his answer to be.

He stroked my hair with his free hand. "You make me want to try."

Those six little words filled me with hope and scared me shitless.

"You're not the only one who's afraid." I might have been long over Jared, but the aftershocks of his betrayal still stung. Not only that, but he was also just someone else who didn't want me.

"What are you afraid of?" he asked.

My truth ripped open wounds that ran soul deep, and we weren't going to talk about that. No longer able to meet his gaze, I looked away. Covering my mouth, I attempted to stifle a yawn.

Tucker kissed my forehead. "Sleep. We'll talk tomorrow."

Glad for the reprieve and completely exhausted, I rolled over and closed my eyes. Tucker draped an arm over my hip, tugging me flush against him, and I drifted off.

The next morning, I woke to find myself alone, except for Tucker's scent that clung to the pillow he'd slept on. I scanned the room for a sign, something that told me I was wrong. My eyes paused on the dresser. Tucker's clothes were gone. Aside from the electrical buzz of the refrigerator and the whir from the air conditioner, the house was utterly silent. He'd left, and I hated how my heart sank at the knowledge.

I got up, took a shower, brushed my teeth, and threw on a T-shirt and shorts. Then, a thought occurred to me. Maybe his mom had called. I grasped at the straw like a lifeline and let my imagination run wild. Because, if something had come up, it would mean that Tucker had left because he needed to, not because he didn't want me. Then, my imagination ran a little too far.

What if something was wrong with Shayne?

All the moments she and I'd shared began to spin in my head. Cartwheels and round-offs on the lawn. How disappointed she had been to learn I didn't possess magical powers. Her first day of school—a memory that shouldn't even belong to me but did. Regardless of what had transpired between me and Tucker, I had to know Shayne was okay. Because, somewhere along the line, my not-quite-six-year-old neighbor had become one of my favorite humans, and as pathetic as it sounded, aside from Grayson, Shayne was probably my best friend.

Propelled by concern for a child who wasn't mine, I tore through the house, looking for my purse, which was the last place I remembered having my phone. After I looked for a full five minutes, I found my purse in the living room. While I dug through it, I looked out the window. Tucker's truck wasn't in his driveway, and I wasn't sure if it made me feel better or worse. I was two seconds from dumping the contents of my bag when I finally unearthed my cell, buried at the bottom. I swiped my finger over the black screen, and nothing happened.

"For fuck's sake," I shouted at the shiny rectangle.

Either I needed a new battery or to at least remember to plug the damn thing in to charge. I headed into the kitchen to connect the phone to one of the four charger ports scattered throughout the house. One might think a person who had so many of them would remember to use them.

I snapped the hair tie off my wrist and gathered my hair in a topknot.

Coffee. I needed coffee.

I'd wait for my phone to charge and then call Tucker. More than likely, everything was completely fine. Hopefully, the coffee would take the edge off the crazy.

Inhaling a calming breath, I opened the cabinet above the coffee pot and took out the small grinder and the bag of beans. Some people may consider it ridiculous to go to all that trouble for a cup of joe, but I was one of those rare birds who didn't own a Keurig. There was just something about the scent of freshly ground beans that soothed the soul. How the aroma wafted in the air, bringing memories along with it. At thirteen, when most kids received makeup or gaming systems for their birthdays, my dad had bought me a coffee mug and a Scrabble board game. Both of which I still had. It was one of the best birthdays I'd ever had.

I just finished adding the grounds to the filter and filling the reservoir with water when the front door swung open. There was only one person it could be, and I gave him my back because I wasn't ready to turn around just yet. I was a pathetic mess, and I needed to get my shit together.

He came back. Shayne is fine.

Tucker's voice filled the space between us. "You're awake," he stated the obvious.

I pressed the start button on the pot, plastered a smile on my face, and pivoted to face him. Clutched in his hands were two medium-sized white paper bags with a sunflower printed on them. Scrawled in loopy script, it read *Crystal Creek Bakery Company*.

"Breakfast?" I quirked a brow. "So, that's where you were. That's so sweet." It would've been a hell of a lot sweeter if he'd left my needy ass a note.

"Where did you think I went?" He was wearing jeans and an olive-green T-shirt that complemented his gorgeous eyes.

That was a loaded question. The only thing I hadn't considered was the possibility that he went to get breakfast. When I'd woken up in an empty bed, I'd just known he was gone. Maybe it had been too much for him. Maybe he'd changed his mind and decided he didn't want to try this after all.

Without answering, I reached into the cabinet for a mug and put the grinder back. "Do you want a cup?"

"Sure." He started unloading the contents of the bag onto the island while I swapped the pot out to fill his mug and repeated the process with mine.

"Here." I passed Tucker his coffee cup.

He took a sip, set it aside, and began opening containers to reveal a continental breakfast spread. Berries, bagels, muffins, granola, yogurt, and a few other things.

"Isn't this a lot of food for two people?"

He shrugged. "I didn't know what you wanted. Sit. Eat."

"Thank you. This is very thoughtful." I reached for a muffin.

Tucker raked a hand through his hair and rubbed the

back of his neck. "Camryn, are you okay? You seem a little ... off."

"I'm fine," I said and took a bite of banana nut muffin to conceal my lie. But there wasn't room in my mouth for both, and the cakey substance grew thick. I picked up my coffee and took a big gulp, which made me start choking.

Tucker quickly moved into action. He ripped off a paper towel, shoved it into my palm, and began to rub circles between my shoulder blades.

My eyes stung with tears. "Water," I stammered.

He grabbed a bottle from the fridge, twisted off the cap, and gave it to me.

It took a few minutes for me to calm down, but eventually, I got myself under control.

"Babe, tell me what's wrong."

"When I woke up, you were gone."

"I went to get breakfast." His brow lifted. "Wait. You thought I'd just left?"

My silence was all the conformation he needed

"After last night, you think I, what? Used you for sex?"

In three seconds, my crazy was coming out to play, and I needed a little bit of space. Without looking up, I walked past him. If he kept pushing, it was all going to come out like word vomit.

"Do you really think I'm that much of an asshole?"

I set my water on the coffee table and then twisted to face him. "Last night, you said sex was a lot less complicated. What was I supposed to think? You never left a note." Those abandonment issues I knew I had but swore I didn't? This was the universe calling bullshit. "And, no, Tucker, I don't think you're that much of an asshole. I started to rationalize that maybe your mom had called or Shayne was sick or something had happened. Then, I felt like a crazy person because, if something had happened, it would mean that you hadn't left by choice. I was going to call you, but per usual, my phone was dead. I plugged it in and started a pot of coffee. In all those scenarios, never once did I consider you'd just gone to grab breakfast."

And there it was—the crux of all my fears. My hand flew over my mouth, as if I could capture all the words and swallow them back. This was exactly why I tried so hard not to let anyone in. There was your normal run-of-the-mill crazy, but everything I'd just unloaded on Tucker went far beyond that.

He opened his mouth and then shut it. Then, he opened it again. He looked like a damn guppy.

21

TUCKER

I stared at Camryn, dumbfounded expression fixed on my face, and tried to figure out what to say.

During her little rampage, I'd realized a few things. One, I'd had no idea she was so animated when she lost her shit. It was fucking adorable, but I decided to keep that to myself. Two, her abandonment issues ran deeper than I'd known. And, three, I'd just fallen in love with her.

"Say something."

Words tumbled in my head like change in a dryer. I didn't want to say the wrong thing. I wanted to make it better. I knew this wasn't Camryn being dramatic. Aside from her father, everyone else had tossed her away, and she expected me to do the same.

"Okay, let me help you," she said. "*Camryn, the sex was amazing, but you're a whole can of crazy—and not the fun kind.*" She held up a finger. "Wait, I've got it." Clearing her throat, she said, "*Camryn, on second thought, it really was just sex.*"

That one pissed me off. She didn't get to say that shit and then put space between us, so I stalked into the living room.

"Enough." I took her hand, sat on the couch, and pulled her onto my lap.

My hands dived into her hair, ridding her of the tie that secured it. Her damp, dark hair fell down her back. I gathered it, wound the strands in my fist, and gently tugged her head.

Gorgeous eyes stared up at me. A man could get fucking lost in those baby blues.

"Camryn, the sex was amazing." Kiss. "There will be a next time." Kiss. "It was a whole lot of things, baby. But just sex? Not a fucking chance," I growled that last part.

I kissed my way along her jaw to her lips. She opened on a moan, and I plunged my tongue inside, waging a war against her mouth. When I was certain she was convinced, I released her hair and placed my hands on her hips.

Her flattened palms lying against my chest, she picked at the imaginary lint, refusing to look at me. "I'm sorry I kind of freaked out. I'm fine."

"Is that how you think this works? That you can tell me you're fine, and I'm going to believe you? I saw that look on your face. This is me trying, but I can't be the only one in this, Camryn."

I stilled her hands, but her eyes remained fixed on my shirt. This wasn't easy for her, and as much as I wanted her to look at me, I wanted her words more.

She blew out a hard breath. "If I'm sleeping, just leave me a note. Or you can wake me up. Shoot me a text. Send a fucking carrier pigeon. Just don't disappear."

Her pain sliced through me, leaving me gutted. I lifted her wrist to my lips, planting a tender kiss to the inside.

"Okay, baby."

"God, that makes me sound so needy, and I hate it." She

dropped her head to my chest and wrapped her arms around my neck.

"I like you needy," I told her, trailing my hand over her back.

Dick hard as a fucking rock, I carried her back to bed. With every stroke of my cock, I intended to erase all her doubts from the inside out.

22

CAMRYN

Over the next several weeks, Tucker, Shayne, and I began to spend more and more time together. Each day, I fell a little more for him. We took advantage of stolen moments whenever we could. Enjoying dates when Shayne spent the night with Tucker's mom, whom I'd yet to meet. I knew he was being cautious, and we both had our own issues to overcome. We kept the public displays of affection to a minimum in front of Shayne, though it was only a matter of time before that was no longer possible. The kid was too smart for her own good. I adored her, and she already owned a piece of my heart. That was why, when Tucker sent me a text one Friday afternoon, asking me if I minded picking up Shayne from the garage, I was happy to do it.

The lobby was empty when I walked inside, except for Nash, who stood behind the high counter. The door chimed, and he looked up.

"Hey, Nash."

"Camryn. Nice to see you again."

We'd bumped into Nash and Macy at the park last week, but I hadn't seen either of them since.

"Where's Shayne?"

"She's hanging out with Macy at her office. Tuck had to go pick up a part, but he'll be right back."

"Oh. Okay. Well, I'll go visit with the girls, and we'll come back in a few," I told him and turned to go.

"Camryn, hold up."

I stopped and pivoted back to him.

"Do you have a second?" He folded his arms over his chest.

"Sure. What's up?"

"Tucker is my best friend, and he's been through hell."

I nodded, not entirely certain what he was hinting at.

"He looks happy. Happier than he has in a long fucking time."

"That's a good thing, right? Seeing your friend happy."

"I haven't decided."

"What does that even mean? Nash, if you've got something to say, just say it."

"What's your plan?"

"Excuse me?"

What the hell is his problem?

"If you're just using him to pass time—"

"Stop right there." I held a hand up, palm out. "I get that I'm new in town, and we haven't really had a chance to get to know each other." My eyes shifted to the cement floor before they lifted to meet his gaze. "You're just going to have to trust me when I say, that isn't the kind of person that I am. I've grown to care about not only Tucker, but Shayne as well. Whatever this thing is between me and Tucker, it's exactly that—between me and him."

Intense and unyielding, his eyes bored into me. I met his stare and held my ground.

After a minute that felt more like an hour, Nash spoke, "That might be true, but if this thing between you two goes south, who do you think is going to help him get his shit together again? Not to mention, Shayne seems pretty damn attached."

"If you think I hold all the power, that Tucker is the only one at risk of being hurt, then you don't know a damn thing. Because, if this thing between us goes south"—I used his phrase against him—"he has you. And Shayne and his mom and Macy. I have nobody Nash. Not that it's your business, but my dad raised me alone. My circumstances might have been different, but I've been in Shayne's shoes. This isn't a game to me. I care about them both." My feelings ran deeper that, but I kept it to myself.

Nash's hard look softened. "Such a fucking asshole," he muttered. "I'm such a fucking asshole. Camryn, I'm sorry. You're the first person he's let get close since ..." His voice trailed off.

"I understand, and I appreciate that you want to look out for your friend. But Tucker is a big boy, and I don't plan on going anywhere. Thank you for the apology."

"You really do care about them."

"Yeah, I do."

The door sounded, and Tucker walked inside with a box clutched in his hands. "Hey, beau—" He stopped mid-greeting, eyes flitting back and forth between me and Nash. "What's going on?"

"Nothing," Nash spoke up. "We were just having a chat."

"Uh-huh." Tucker set the package down on the counter, came to stand in front of me, and planted a quick peck on my lips. "Everything all right?" He side-eyed Nash.

"Yeah. It's all good."

He gave a slight nod, but I knew the conversation wasn't over.

"Where's Bug?"

As if summoned by the mere mention of her name, Shayne barreled through the door, Macy on her heels.

Tucker took a step back, the action not fazing me in the least. We were taking things very slow in front of Shayne.

"Camryn," she squealed. Arms wide open, Shayne threw herself into me.

"Hi, sweet girl." I bent to give her a half-hug, her body still clinging to my waist.

"I missed you." Her words bloomed a tenderness inside me.

"I just saw you at school earlier though."

"That's different," she declared, taking a step back and planting her hands on her hips. "At school, you're Miss Parker. Not at school, you're my friend."

"You know what?"

"What?"

"You're seriously my favorite human."

"You're mine, too. Well, except for Daddy."

Tucker and I both chuckled. I shifted my focus from Shayne to the adults in the room. Macy grinned like a fool while Nash seemed more subdued. I couldn't fault him for being protective of his best friend.

"Macy, how are you?" I asked.

"Great. Are we still on for drinks tomorrow?"

"Absolutely. The Hideaway at seven, right?"

"Yes, ma'am." Macy turned her attention to Shayne. "Come give me a hug. I have to get back to the office to close up."

Macy bent down for Shayne to wrap her arms around her neck.

"Love you, Aunt Macy."

"Love you, too, Butter Bean."

A chorus of good-byes ushered Macy out the door.

"We should get going, too," I said to Tucker.

He nodded. "Nash, I'll be right back, man. I'm going to help Camryn with the car seat."

Nash came out from behind the counter, scooped Shayne up in a hug, and pretended to eat her neck.

Shayne squirmed and shrieked with giggles. "Uncle Nash, stop it."

He kissed the top of her head. "Love you, Monkey," he said and set her down.

"Love you, too." Shayne's small hand slipped in mine. "Come on, Camryn. Let's get out of here."

The three of us strode toward the door.

"Good night, Nash," I called over my shoulder.

"Have a good one, Camryn."

After Tucker installed the car seat and made sure Shayne had buckled herself in, he came to where I stood outside the driver's door.

"He was giving you shit, wasn't he?"

I folded my arms over my chest and rocked on my heels. "Not really. He's looking out for you; that's all."

"What did he say to you?" Tucker's jaw twitched.

"Nothing I couldn't handle."

"Camryn."

"Really, Tucker, it's fine. He basically just said you don't let people get too close, and it wasn't something I should take lightly."

"Nosy bastard."

"Maybe, but you're lucky to have him."

"I'd better get back. Thanks for taking care of Shayne."

A warmth spread through me. The fact that Tucker trusted me with his daughter meant more to me than he knew. "Of course."

Tucker reached for my hand and squeezed it. "I'll see you later."

"Bye," I said and then climbed into the car.

We waved to him as we pulled out of the parking lot and headed for home.

I glanced in the rearview mirror to look at Shayne. "Guess what, kiddo? I have a surprise for you."

"You do?"

"Yep." I focused back on the road.

"I can't wait. What is it?"

"Nice try. You'll find out soon enough."

Shayne offered up random guesses as we made our way back home. By the time we pulled into the driveway, she could barely contain her excitement. She unfastened her seat belt and made a beeline for the door.

"Are you ready to have some fun?" I asked while I unlocked the door.

"Yes."

"All right, kick your shoes off, and let's head to the kitchen."

I threw my purse on the coffee table and fell into step behind a shoeless Shayne. The contents of the grocery store baking aisle was fanned out across the counter. Strawberry cake mix, powdered sugar for frosting, and an array of sprinkles were among them.

Wide-eyed elation spanned Shayne's features. "We're making cupcakes?"

"We sure are."

"You're so good at surprises."

"Why, thank you." I curtsied, which made her giggle. "All right, so there are a few rules."

"Rules?" She looked puzzled. "Wait. We still get to have fun, right?"

"Yes."

She nodded her head in agreement. "I'm all ears."

"First, we're going to put our hair up; that way, it doesn't fall into the food." I reached into the kitchen junk drawer where I'd stashed a few elastics. Quickly, I whipped my hair into a messy bun and then did the same with Shayne's.

"Second?" she asked, keeping us on task.

"We need to wash our hands." I moved the step stool in front of the sink and turned on the water.

Shayne climbed up, and together, we washed and dried our hands.

"Rule number three"—I stooped to be eye-level with her because it was the most important one of them all—"you may not touch the oven."

She stuck her hand out and said in a serious tone, "I accept these rules."

I laughed and put my hand in hers. "Here, let's put this on." I snatched the aprons I'd placed on the counter earlier. "Do you want the one with cupcakes on it or doughnuts?"

"Hmm ..." She crooked her forefinger and tapped her chin. "Cupcakes."

"Excellent choice." I slipped it over her head and tied it around her waist twice because it was entirely too big. Then, I put on the other one. "While I start the batter, you can put the paper cups in the muffin tins."

I lifted Shayne and set her on top of the island. Then, I opened the small canister of cupcake liners. While she was busy with that, I preheated the oven and began measuring out water and then oil. Then, I cracked the eggs.

"All done," she announced.

"You want to help me mix?"

She bobbed her head.

"Just make sure you keep the beaters in the bowl; otherwise, the mess will be all over the kitchen."

I plugged the hand mixer into the outlet. With my hands positioned on top of Shayne's, we blended the batter according to the directions on the box. Afterward, we divided it between the wells, and I popped the pans into the oven.

"Here you go." Pink goop dripped from the beater as I passed it to her.

Her small tongue darted out to capture the wayward sweetness. "This is delectable," she said, rolling her eyes to the back of her head.

I couldn't help but laugh. Her antics and vocabulary made her seem like an adult in a kid's body.

"Agreed." I brought the other beater to my mouth. "After the cupcakes cool, we'll decorate them. That's the best part."

"Did you buy frosting?"

"No, because we're going to make that, too." There was little I hated more than store-bought frosting.

"We are?"

"Yep."

"What a mess we made." Shayne glanced at the space around us.

"We did, but we'll clean it up."

I pilfered two clean dishrags from the drawer by the sink. I wet one, and after I wrung it out, I gave it to Shayne. "You can start wiping off the counter while I take care of the dishes, and then we'll whip up the frosting." I helped her down and shifted the stool over to the island.

By the time we had restored order, the oven timer chirped.

"They're done," she announced gleefully.

With oven mitts covering my hands, I reached into the oven and pulled them out. Then, I set them on the stovetop to cool.

"Are we going to make the icing now?"

"Yep." I slid off the thick mitts and went over to her. "Open these and put them in the bowl." I placed two sticks of softened butter in front of her. Then, I went to the fridge for the heavy whipping cream.

My phone rang from the other room.

"Hang on, that's probably your dad. Don't move." I retrieved my cell from the abyss of my purse and accepted the call. Then, I returned to the kitchen.

"Hey, baby," he said low into the phone.

"Hi."

"Everything okay?"

"We're good."

"Hi, Daddy!" Shayne yelled to Tucker.

He chuckled. "Tell her hello."

"Your dad says hi back." I smiled.

"I should be done here in a little while."

"No problem. I was going to order pizza for dinner if you two want to stay."

We ate together a few times a week, but there was no set schedule.

"Tell you what. I'll pick it up."

"Just remember, no black olives."

"I remember. See you soon." The deep timbre of his voice washed over me, and I couldn't wait to see him.

"Bye." I ended the call and looked at Shayne. "Where were we?"

She pointed to the bowl.

"Next, we need powdered sugar." I pointed to the bag.

Over the next several minutes, we finished our task and divided the white fluff between four small bowls. With my help, Shayne added food coloring to them.

"We need some music," I told her.

After I wiped my hands on my apron, I reached for my phone and scrolled through the playlists. When I found what I was looking for, I tapped the screen. "Glory Days" by Bruce Springsteen filled the kitchen. Shayne bobbed her head to the tune. Since the cakes were cool, I carried the pans over to our work surface and freed them. Then, I snatched several butter knives from the silverware drawer and a couple of small rubber spatulas from the utensil canister, laying them alongside the cupcakes.

"Grab one and start decorating, kiddo."

"I'm going to make a pink one with pink sparkles," she proclaimed, reaching for a cupcake. Tongue tucked into the corner of her mouth, a look of deep concentration on her face, she frosted her first one.

A sense of wonder filled me as I watched her. She was amazing. And, looking at her, I knew I wanted this. Not because I was trying to fill some void left in my life. I didn't just want a family. I wanted them, and it scared the hell out of me. Because I wasn't the girl who got what she wanted. I wasn't even the girl who got the consolation prize.

"Camryn, aren't you going to make one?" Shayne asked, her smile huge.

It was enough to snap me out of my melancholy. "Of course," I said and reached for a cupcake and the blue frosting.

We worked in silence for a few minutes—that was, until

the thump of "Girls Just Want to Have Fun" spilled into the air.

"Oh, Shayne. Do you know what time it is?" Excitement filled my voice.

"No." She looked at me like I'd lost my mind.

"It's dance-party time." I went around to her side of the counter, scooped her off the stool, and then reached for the goop-covered spatulas we'd been using. "Your microphone, my lady," I said, giving her one.

She giggled and accepted the gift I'd just bestowed upon her. Whenever "Girls Just Want to Have Fun" came on, you danced your ass off, and you sang the lyrics at the top of your voice. It was girl code, Sisterhood 101.

In our messy aprons, we bopped our heads and shook our backsides all around the kitchen. By the time the chorus came around again, Shayne had the words down. Facing each other, we sang extra loud to make up for the fact that our microphones didn't amplify our voices.

23

TUCKER

I rapped on the door and then stood on the porch for a full two minutes. That was how long it took me to realize that nobody had heard me. In a circus-like balancing act, I managed to open it. Quite a feat, considering my arms grasped pizza boxes, chocolate milk, and a six-pack of beer.

Music hit my ears as I stepped through the entryway. I caught sight of my two girls as they danced like fools in the kitchen and figured that was the reason Camryn never answered.

They sang loudly and a little off-key into frosting-covered objects, completely oblivious to my presence. The corners of my mouth tipped up. Their profiles were to me, as Camryn faced Shayne. Fake microphones between them, heads nearly touching, they shouted the last line of the iconic song like a declaration.

As the music faded, Shayne spread her arms wide and wrapped them around Camryn's waist, squeezing her tight. "I love you, Camryn."

Everything evaporated into the background. I was unable to inhale or exhale, the air in my lungs unexpectedly trapped. Seconds, maybe centuries, passed before Camryn's arms folded around my daughter. I watched her swallow past the lump in her throat.

"I love you, too, sweet girl."

Like the hooked end of a pry bar, Camryn's confession dug into the deepest part of me. The walls around my heart splintered. I didn't want to love her, but it was too late. I was a fucking goner.

Slowly, I raised a foot to kick the door shut. The sound was loud enough to garner their attention.

"Daddy!" Shayne yelled. Arms extended, imaginary mic in her grip, she ran at me.

I braced myself for the impact, but before Shayne could fly into me full force, I said the one word I knew would stop her in her tracks, "Freeze."

She skidded to a halt, posing like a statue. "Let me set this stuff down, Doodlebug, and then I'll give you a hug."

She didn't move or say a word because she was frozen.

"Tucker, I'm sorry. Let me help you," Camryn offered.

"No worries. I've got it." I kept my voice light despite my heavy realization seconds earlier. "Looks like you two were having fun." I deposited the food and drinks on the empty counter near the sink.

"You might want to unfreeze her." Camryn smiled and pointed to Shayne.

"In a second." My tone was low.

I pulled Camryn close. Since Shayne was facing the door and couldn't see us, I gave Camryn a quick peck on the lips and then stepped back to put a few feet between us. I wasn't sure how much longer I'd be able to do that.

"Unfreeze, Doodlebug."

She squealed and raced into the kitchen. I scooped her up for a hug, and she wrapped her legs around me.

"Did you have fun with Camryn?"

Shayne leaned back in my arms, so she could see my face. "So much fun. We made cupcakes. And frosting. Lots of different frosting." She looked thoughtful. "Well ... really, it was one frosting, but we made different colors. Oh, and sprinkles. But we didn't make those. Camryn already bought them. Lots of them. Rainbow ones and pink ones and shimmery glitter ones, but the kind you can eat. Not like we use at school. My teacher, Mrs. Jenkins, says glitter is the devil. One day, my friend Wyatt spilled it all over the place, and then Mrs. Jenkins was so unnerved."

"Take a breath, Bug." I chuckled and looked at Camryn.

She stood there, a smile on her face, deep longing in her eyes. Something in that look broke me and healed me at the same time. I wanted her. She needed us. Without any regard for the repercussions, I shifted Shayne to my side, held her in one arm, and opened the other to Camryn.

She hesitated, and I heard the questions she didn't ask.

"Come on, Camryn," Shayne prodded while opening her arm to mimic my stance. "We can have a group hug."

Glassy-eyed Camryn stepped into our embrace. We were a tangle of arms. The two of them in their frosting-spattered aprons and me with the traces of grease that remained on my shirt. Countless seconds passed as we held each other close.

"I'm hungry," Shayne said, her voice muffled between my shoulder and Camryn's forehead. Her words reminded me of the pizza growing cold on the counter and the beer and milk getting warm.

Camryn broke the connection and took a step back. She moved to the island and said over her shoulder, "I'll just get this cleaned up really quick, and then we'll eat." Her voice quaked, and it didn't take a genius to figure out the moment had affected her.

I set Shayne on her feet. "Let's get this off you, and then you need to go wash your hands." I made quick work of her apron and sent her on her way.

Once she was in the bathroom, I put the milk and beer in the fridge and then closed in on Camryn. I untied her apron and set it to the side. With my front pressed to her back, my arms encircled her waist, holding her against me. I planted kisses to the back of her neck.

"You okay?"

She didn't lean into my touch, but she didn't pull away either.

"Talk to me."

"It's nothing. I just need a minute."

I wanted to push her. To make her tell me what was going on inside that head of hers.

Then, Shayne's voice rang out from the other room. "*Daa-dee.*"

"I'm going to go check on her. But this conversation isn't over." Then again, it never really started.

Camryn didn't have to spell it out for me. I knew she was scared. She wasn't alone in that. I was fucking terrified.

"*Daa-dee!*" Shayne hollered again, louder this time.

I kissed the back of Camryn's head and went to tend to my daughter.

Shayne was pacing in front of the bathroom door.

"Bug, what's the matter?"

"I had to poop." She nervously looked around.

"Okay. You've been taking care of that on your own for a while now. What's the problem?"

"Well ... the potty is, um ... full." She twisted her hands together.

"What do you mean, it's full?" I suspiciously eyed her.

Shayne had never been the kind of kid to screw around in the bathroom.

She crooked her finger and motioned for me to come closer. I knelt, so we were eye-level.

She put her hands on my shoulders, and in an extremely serious tone, she said, "Daddy, we have a situation. I had to make a big poop, and I flushed the toilet, but the potty doesn't want it. It won't swallow my poop."

It took everything I had not to roll on the floor and laugh hysterically. I rubbed a hand over my jaw and struggled to keep it together. "Bug, it's fine. I'll fix it. Did you wash your hands?"

She rolled her eyes. "Of course I washed my hands."

"Don't roll your eyes at me. Go help Camryn clean up while I take care of this."

"All right."

She skipped away, and I opened the bathroom door.

Thankfully, there was a plunger behind the garbage can. Shayne wasn't kidding. The size of that thing was impressive. How she hadn't complained of a stomachache, I didn't know.

By the time I took care of everything, washed up, and made it back to the kitchen, Camryn had most of the mess cleaned up. The cupcakes sat on a platter in the center of the island. She had the pizza plated and was mid-pour of a glass of chocolate milk for Shayne.

"Everything okay?" Camryn asked when her eyes lifted.

"It's all taken care of." I smirked.

"I thought we could eat in the living room. Maybe watch a movie."

"Can we watch *Beauty and the Beast*?" Shayne clasped her hands together. "Please?"

"Bug, we've watched it at least a hundred times in the last month. How about something else?"

"I'm good with *Beauty and the Beast*," Camryn agreed. "It's on the DVR."

Shayne raised a fist, and Camryn gave it a pound.

"Girl power," Shayne proclaimed.

Camryn went to turn on the television while I grabbed our plates and the two beers, and Shayne carried her milk. We curled up on the sofa with my daughter between us. The girls watched the screen, caught up in the movie. However, I lost myself in watching them.

Shayne sang, but Camryn mouthed the words to the songs. Halfway through the movie, Shayne laid her head on the throw pillow Camryn had on her lap. Camryn freed Shayne's hair from the knot it had been in and carefully combed her fingers through it. Minutes later, Shayne was softly snoring, and I closed my eyes.

"Tucker," Camryn whispered. "Tucker."

"Hmm?"

Fingertips grazed my bicep. I blinked a few times and then finally focused on Camryn's face.

"I have to pee." She pointed to the sleeping body on her lap.

It was a beautiful sight.

"Tucker," Camryn whisper-yelled, "I have to pee!"

Realization finally set in. "Shit, I'm sorry, babe."

Carefully, I stood and then leaned down to lift Shayne off Camryn. We managed the task without waking her. Camryn scurried to the bathroom while I snagged another beer from the fridge. A few minutes later, she wandered into the kitchen. I set my beer down and pulled her into my arms.

"You know, it wasn't cool that you sided with the little

tyrant. The song about Gaston gets stuck in my head for days. What is the obsession with that damn movie?"

"It's an incredible love story, and the Beast gives her a library," she said matter-of-factly.

"And?"

"Haven't you heard?" she asked with a laugh. "Bitches love libraries."

"I'll have to remember that."

We stood in a wordless embrace. Her head rested over my heart, and my chin rested on her crown. Several long minutes passed, and I needed to know what she had been thinking earlier. She'd had more than a minute. When I couldn't take it anymore, I broke the silence. It was time to demand answers.

24

CAMRYN

Tucker captured my chin between his thumb and index finger and tilted my face upward to meet his gaze. "Talk to me."

Such a simple command, but there wasn't anything simple about it. So many feelings collided within me, and I wasn't sure I could put them into words. His lips met mine in a soft, tender, coaxing kiss.

"Talk to me," he repeated.

Maybe, if I told him, it would be easier.

"I'm scared." My confession sounded weak, even to my own ears.

His hands found my waist, and he set me on the island. He stood between my legs, large palms on either side, caging me in. Waiting for me to elaborate. When I didn't, he pushed further. "What are you afraid of?"

You. This. Us. Everything.

"Because what if this"—I waved a finger between the two of us—"doesn't work out? People leave. And I'm always the one left behind." The words tumbled out of my mouth, and I hated how pathetic they made me feel.

He bent his lips to mine and tenderly kissed me. Every swipe of his tongue against mine was an unspoken promise I clung to. When he pulled back, his gaze was intense.

"Camryn, I know you're scared, and you're not alone in that, but you're worth the risk. I'm not going anywhere. Okay?"

"Okay," I said, trying like hell to let his words reassure me. I gripped the belt loops on his jeans, tugging him closer, and then I kissed him like my life depended on it.

He groaned against my mouth. "You're killing me, woman." His low growl sent tingles down my spine. "I'd love nothing more than to take you on this counter, but since that's not an option"—he looked to the living room where Shayne lay, sleeping—"meet me on your back porch in ten minutes." His arms came around my waist, and he lifted me off the countertop and set my feet on the floor.

"Where are you going?"

"Home to take a shower, and then I'm coming back to have my wicked way with you."

"But—"

He pressed a finger to my lips, cutting me off. "She's asleep. Ten minutes." He headed out the back door.

I crept down the hall to the bathroom and took the fastest shower of my life. Afterward, I threw on a button-down nightshirt and ran a comb through my towel-dried hair. On my way back into the kitchen, I peeked at Shayne. She was sleeping soundly, and I offered up a silent prayer to every known deity that she'd stay that way.

The cupcakes called out to me, and I snatched one from the platter on my way out the door, leaving it slightly ajar in case Shayne woke up. Tucker rearranged the patio furniture, positioning the cushioned chaise lounge in the shadows where he was waiting for me. He wore a smile on his face and a pair of athletic shorts around his hips.

"Slide that in front of the door." He gestured to the small, round bistro table.

"Good idea." I laughed. Apparently, stolen moments required creativity and booby traps.

"Come here, baby." That deep, gravelly voice tiptoed over my skin.

He extended his hand and pulled me down to straddle him.

I swooped a finger through the creamy frosting, but before I had the chance to lick it off, Tucker seized my wrist.

"Hey, no fair."

I pouted, but then he brought the tip of my finger to his lips and sucked. I was sure I could get off just by watching him. His hard length, coupled with the cool, slinky material of his shorts, had my bare center on sensory overload.

Tucker worked the buttons of my shirt to expose my breasts, and then he stole my cupcake and swirled the remaining frosting over my nipples before casting the cake aside. His mouth was on mine in a flash. Hot, hungry, and so full of need. Just when I thought I'd come from his kiss alone, he ghosted his lips over my jaw to the tender flesh below my earlobe.

Heat pooled in my core. Anticipation thrummed in my veins. "Tucker, please."

"Hold on to the chair." His whispered demand burned hot against my skin. "Don't let go."

An incoherent sound somewhere between a mewl and moan escaped me.

Tucker trailed his finger through the saccharine substance and brought it to my lips. While I sucked his finger clean, he lowered his head and circled his tongue over one nipple and then the other. Teeth scraped, whiskers rubbed. My body blazed with need as he slowly withdrew his finger and trailed it down my body to circle my aching bundle of nerves.

Every second, my need grew more frantic. I cried out as he inserted a finger inside me and added another. "Right there, Tucker. God, yes."

My hands dived into his hair, and I bucked against him. Then, he pulled his mouth away.

"No. Please don't stop," I whimpered at the loss.

"I'm going to take care of you, I promise. Where are your hands supposed to be?" he chided.

The chair ... right, I'm supposed to hold on to it.

With each arm positioned back in place over his shoulders, my fingers gripped the edge. "I won't let go again. Please, Tucker," I begged, writhing against him like some wanton creature.

"I've got you." He started the sweet torture all over again. Nipping, licking, and sucking. Once again, he slipped his hand low between my legs.

My back arched into him. "God, you feel so good."

The pad of his thumb rubbed slow circles over my clit. Sounds I didn't even recognize as my own fell from my lips.

"You like that, don't you? You're so wet for me." He strummed over my clit. "I need you to come for me, baby." His hot, hungry words hit my ears. One hand moved to the back of my neck while the other continued the most divine torture.

"Oh God," I moaned.

He sucked my nipple hard between his teeth and pinched my clit at the same time. I detonated in his hand.

My hands gripped his biceps, nails biting into his flesh. He crashed his mouth over mine, swallowing my screams as the orgasm rocketed through me. Stars burst behind my eyes. A sheen of sweat covered my body, and I knew I would never look at cupcakes the same way again.

25

TUCKER

Camryn remained on my lap. Hair disheveled, moonlight spilling over her bare tits, a smile on her face, post-orgasmic haze in her eyes. She was absolute perfection, and I wanted to bury myself inside her for days.

I lightly kissed her, our frenzied movements from minutes ago replaced with tenderness. My tongue slipped past her lips, dipping into her mouth. Every stroke of my tongue against hers was an unspoken confession. I tightly wrapped my arms around her, breaking the seal of our lips, hugging her to my chest. My lips pressed against her hair, and I wanted to say the words, to tell her how much I loved her. That I'd never been in love like this, and that was the truth.

Holly and I had both been young, desperate to get out of this town and see the world, but the love we had once shared wasn't the kind that held on when everything fell apart. As much as I loved Dani and missed her every single day; she was gone. Dani was my past, and I wanted Camryn to be my future. She was selfless and kind, and she loved with her whole heart even though it scared her to death.

"We should go inside," I told her.

"But you didn't …" she stammered. "I mean, I need to take care of you."

Damn, this woman was killing me.

"Baby, it's not about tit for tat. Tonight is all about you." I squeezed her ass. "Come on, let's go inside and clean up."

Reluctantly, Camryn got off my lap and stood, buttoning her nightshirt over her bare chest. I grabbed my T-shirt I'd thrown over a chair earlier, and together, we made our way inside the house. Shayne was snoring softly on the couch as we walked by. Once inside the bathroom, I closed the door, pitched my shirt on the sink, and started the shower.

"You're taking a shower? Now?" She raised a brow.

"No. We're taking a shower." I stalked toward her, and my hands went for the buttons on her nightshirt. Slowly, I began undoing them one by one. My knuckles skated along Camryn's warm skin as I worked my way down.

"But what if she wakes up?"

"She won't," I assured her.

"But what if—"

I cut her words off with a kiss. "She won't."

I stripped out of my shorts and then eased the nightshirt from Camryn's shoulders, down her arms, letting it fall to the tiled floor where it pooled at her feet. My cock grew hard at the sight of her bare before me. I took her by the hand and tugged her under the warm spray of the shower.

With her back to my front, I moved her hair out of the way, dipped my head low, and nipped the sensitive skin on her neck.

She arched her neck and moaned. "That feels so good."

I wanted her lips, so I turned her to face me. A strand of black hair streaked with pink clung to her cheek.

"You have frosting in your hair." I chuckled, brushing it away before dropping my mouth to hers.

The water ran in rivulets over us while I kissed her long and slow, growing stiffer by the second. If I didn't pull away, I'd end up taking her against the wall of the shower, which would be fine, but the shower wasn't exactly huge, and I knew from experience that it took some maneuvering. Not to mention, I wanted her in her bed.

I ended the kiss, reached for the bottle of soap tucked into the nook, and grabbed the netted puff beside it. I poured the liquid onto the thing she used in place of a washcloth and worked it into a lather. The smell of honey and orange blossoms filled the air. I gripped her hair, gently tugging it back, exposing her neck, and nipped the sensitive skin before washing it.

Camryn's fingers dug into my biceps. I released her hair, working my way down her body, paying special attention to her breasts, rubbing circles over her pert nipples. Her hands went to my shoulders as I lowered myself to my knees, soaping up her stomach before moving on to each leg. I skimmed the sponge between her legs before planting a kiss to her wet center.

"Tucker." The desire was evident in her voice. She gripped my hair, trying to gain purchase, as I nudged her legs apart, spread her wide, and dragged my tongue over her heated core, reveling in her sweet taste.

I wrapped an arm around her waist to steady her while I brought her to the edge. She pressed her hips against my mouth, seeking friction. I could feel how close she was, but I wanted to draw it out, so I backed off and stood.

"Why did you stop?" She pouted in frustration.

"So greedy, baby." I kissed her hard, letting her taste

herself on my tongue. "Let's finish up before the water gets cold."

"I sort of hate you right now," she said, squirting shampoo into her palm.

You love me. The thought reverberated in my head, and I hoped like hell it was true.

"Keep telling yourself that," I joked, trying to cover up everything I was feeling.

Camryn rinsed her hair and then reached for the soap. Foam-covered hands roamed over my body, trailing down to my very erect cock. She gripped my shaft, her fingers not quite long enough to meet as she stroked up and down.

I placed a flattened palm against the wall to brace myself. "Damn, baby."

Water cascaded over my body. She licked the droplets, her mouth moving lower as she bent, taking me inside. With her hands on my hips, I fisted her wet hair, guiding her movements. She hollowed out her cheeks, humming around me. When I was seconds away from coming undone, Camryn withdrew her mouth.

She righted herself, grinning like the Cheshire cat. "You know what they say ... payback's a bitch," she said, reaching for the bathrobe hanging from a hook just outside the shower and then stepping out.

I turned off the water and pulled back the curtain. "Baby, you have no idea."

Camryn held two towels. She passed me one and used the other to wrap her hair, turban-style. I stepped out of the tub and fixed the towel around my hips. Steam filled the bathroom, fogging up the mirror.

My eyes bored into her. "I'll give you a head start."

"For what?"

"To run."

She took a step back. "But Shayne."

"I guess you'd better be quiet then."

"Tucker"—she smiled and shook her head—"this is a really bad idea."

"One."

"Wait." She held up a finger.

"Two."

She opened the bathroom door, and her bare feet slapped against the hardwood as she raced down the hall and into her bedroom. I grabbed my clothes and went after her. Once inside her room, I closed the door and listened to make sure our antics hadn't woken Shayne. When I didn't hear anything, I stalked across the room to Camryn. Her eyes moved over the space, looking for somewhere to hide.

I lunged for her, picked her up, and dropped her on the bed. She shrieked, and I pressed a hand over her mouth.

"I believe you said something about payback." My hands went to the belt that cinched her robe, untying it. "You have to be quiet," I reminded her, lifting my hand away. Then, I tickled her.

"Tucker. Tucker, stop." She giggled, trying to get away from me. Her robe fell open as we rolled around on her bed, both laughing like fools. "Mercy. Uncle," she cried.

I pinned her wrists over her head. Camryn's eyes lit with happiness. Her cheeks were pink, and I knew it had nothing to do with the hot shower. She squirmed against my hold, that gorgeous smile of hers possessing me.

The words, "I love you," fell from my lips.

She stopped moving. Stopped smiling. "What?" she whispered.

"You heard me. I love you, Camryn Parker. I'm in love with you, and I have been for a while now."

Tears filled her eyes. "You love me?"

I freed her hands from my grasp to cup her face. "Yes. So fucking much, it hurts."

I nipped her bottom lip before sucking it into my mouth. I kissed her slow and deep, feeling her tears against my skin, tasting their saltiness on my tongue. Leaning my forehead against hers, I waited. Until this moment, I'd had no idea how badly I wanted to hear those words from her.

"I love you, too," she said through her tears.

"Yeah?"

"Yeah. So fucking much, it hurts," she repeated my words back to me.

"God ... baby, what you do to me." I rotated our bodies, so she was on top and rid her of the robe; my towel was already gone. "I need to be inside you."

"Yes, please."

I rolled us back over, stretching to the nightstand for a condom. My smile grew when I saw there were more than a dozen. Good, because I planned on spending the next few hours buried in the woman I loved.

26

CAMRYN

Darkness blanketed the room, and Tucker was sleeping peacefully beside me. It took several seconds for my eyes to adjust to the lack of light. I held my breath as I slowly slid from beneath his arm. Once I had my bearings, I crept over to my dresser, grabbed a T-shirt and a pair of sleep shorts, and then eased the bedroom door open. After I used the bathroom, I tiptoed into the living room to check on Shayne.

Her head was dangling nearly half off the corner of the couch, one arm slung over her eyes while the other hung down, practically touching the floor. How the hell the kid slept like that was beyond me. Since she'd kicked the cover off at some point, I draped it back over her, and after grabbing a bottle of water from the fridge and noting the time on the microwave clock, I returned to my room to crawl back into bed with Tucker.

Just as I replaced the cap on the water and set it on the nightstand, Tucker stirred but didn't wake. I slid under the covers and tried to fall back to sleep, but I couldn't shut my brain off.

"You heard me. I love you ..." The gravelly words he'd spoken earlier repeated in my head.

He had been buried so deep inside me, I couldn't tell where he ended and I began. He'd loved me from the inside out until there were no walls left between us. I'd given him all of me, let myself fall wholly in love with him.

And I knew, way down in the cavernous place where my soul resided, if Tucker ever walked away ... it'd do more than break me. I'd be so irrevocably ruined, there'd be nothing left. A sense of foreboding settled over me. As much as I tried to shake it, to convince my head and my heart to get on the same page, the part of my brain where my memories were stored reminded me of all the reasons to run. When you'd been let down as many times as I had, when the people who were supposed to love you were the ones who abandoned you, it made it that much more difficult to trust your heart.

"Baby, you're thinking too damn loud." Tucker's sexy voice was scratchy with sleep. He rolled onto his side, slipping a hand under my shirt and dragging the rough pads of his fingers lightly over my skin. "Cam, why are you wearing clothes?"

Cam? I couldn't help but grin at his use of the nickname.

"Because I got up to get a drink and to check on Shayne. I assumed, going out there naked would be frowned upon."

"Shit. What time is it?" He was wide awake now.

"Relax." I stifled a giggle. "Around six, I guess. I'm not really sure." I had no idea how long I'd been lying here, awake. "What time does she usually get up?"

"It depends, but she won't be up for a while yet." Tucker leaned on his elbow and propped his head against his palm.

I rolled onto my side to look at him. My eyes adjusted to

the darkness, and I was able to make out the lines of his face.

Tucker removed his other hand from under my shirt. His knuckles grazed across my cheek, pushing away the lock of hair that had fallen across it. I heard the concern in his words when he asked, "What were you thinking about?"

It was a loaded question, one I didn't want to answer honestly. I knew I needed to trust him. Believe in the love we felt for each other. However, history had a way of repeating itself, and it wasn't that I was a pessimist, but I was a realist.

"Just how much I love you." *And how destroyed I'll be when it ends.*

He brushed his lips over mine and then dropped his head back onto the pillow. He took my hand in his, interlocking our fingers. "We'll talk to Shayne when she gets up, but in the meantime ..." He trailed off as he rolled on top of me. His lips went to my neck, and he whispered, "I need to be inside you."

The hungry words floated over my skin, pebbling my nipples and heating my core.

I didn't trust myself to speak. Instead, I arched my hips against him. Tucker crashed his lips over mine, and morning breath be damned, I didn't care. I loved the way our tongues tangled, the scratch of his beard as it rubbed against me. His lips never left mine as we worked together to get my shorts off. Rough hands went to the hem of my shirt, and he broke the kiss to tug it over my head.

Faint light began to trickle into the room around the edge of the blinds covering the window.

On his knees and positioned between my legs, he took in my naked form. "You're so damn beautiful, baby. I'll never get my fill of you."

"Tucker." I met his eyes, silently pleading with him to

understand the words I couldn't say. I needed him to take me. Own me. Fuck me hard and deep, so thoroughly that my brain would get on board. I drank in every inch of him. All the solid contours and planes. The way his magnificent cock jutted out, full and thick, the drop of pre-cum at the tip begging the same way I was.

Tucker's body tensed, the nod of his head barely visible. He didn't order me to tell him what I wanted. What I needed. Because he understood without the words ever leaving my mouth.

"Roll over, baby. Get on your knees, ass up. And, when you can't hold back anymore, use the pillow to muffle your screams."

Relief flowed through me as I followed his command. He stretched over me to the nightstand, reaching for the foil packet. His front to my back, heat radiated from his body, stoking the flame deep in my center. I waited for the telltale tear, but I heard his voice instead. Felt his breath on my skin.

"I'm so fucking in love with you. Trust me to catch you when you fall."

Tears pricked my eyes as he kissed his way down my back and lined his cock up at my entrance.

He dipped a finger inside me, and I heard how wet I was.

I ached at the loss when he withdrew his finger.

"You're the best thing I've ever tasted."

I peered over my shoulder, watching as he licked my essence from his skin. He sheathed his cock, and I waited with bated breath for him to enter me.

"I'm going to give you everything you need."

Tucker pushed inside leisurely. Stretching me, filling me so deliberately, I found myself holding my breath, waiting for him to bottom out.

When he finally did, I let out a moan.

"You have to be quiet," he reminded me.

I pushed back into him, fisting the sheets. Tucker withdrew almost all the way out and gripped my hips before slamming back into me. He set a punishing pacing, driving so hard that I had to brace myself, flattening my palms against the headboard to keep it from slamming into the wall. His thumb circled my clit as he worked me over, playing my body like an instrument and he was a virtuoso.

He thrust a few more times, and I felt myself climbing higher and higher. I was right there, so close. Just as I dropped my face into the pillow, Tucker pinched my clit. A pleasure-filled scream ripped from my throat, the sound muffled by the billowy cotton I'd buried my face into. Seconds later, Tucker quietly growled out his own release, his fingers digging into my flesh so intensely that I knew I'd carry his mark for days.

I wasn't a masochist. In fact, I was the furthest thing from it, but there was just something about having the token of what we shared lingering on my skin. That it was real. Knowing how well he was able to read me, and I trusted him to give me what I needed. Those bruises would serve as a *fuck you* to the doubts that I knew would plague me.

He kissed me between my shoulder blades and pulled out. "I'll be right back."

"Mmhmm," I hummed. As I was completely sated, the lower half of my body collapsed onto the mattress. I closed my eyes, inhaling a deep breath and then letting it go.

"Feel better?" Tucker asked quietly.

I looked at him perched on the end of the bed and knew I could go the rest of my whole life and never tire of looking at him. "Tons." I sat up and pulled the blanket around me.

He reached for my legs, tugging me closer, unhindered by the covers bunching around me.

"Tucker, what are you doing?" I laughed.

"This." He placed an arm around me, leaning in to kiss my temple. "Do you mind throwing some clothes on and making sure the coast is clear? If it is, I'll sneak out the back and then run home to get Bug a fresh outfit."

"What if she's awake?"

"Then, take her into the kitchen and distract her, so I can sneak out the front."

"You've figured it all out, huh?" I smiled and poked him in the ribs. "Why do I feel like a teenager trying not to get caught with a boy in my room?" I laughed.

"We'll talk to her today," he said, reaching for my hand.

"Tucker, she's your daughter, and that's your call to make. If you're not ready—"

"That's just it," he cut me off. "I've been ready, and frankly, I think Bug is, too. I just ..." He trailed off.

"Just what?" I squeezed his hand, urging him to go on.

"You're sure you want this? Not just me ... but her, too?"

"I love you, Tucker, and honestly, I fell for Shayne first." I had no idea what the future had in store, but I knew I wanted it to include the two of them. "I'm all in."

His hand went to the back of my neck, and then he brought his lips to mine, softly kissing me. "We'd better get moving," he said, releasing his hold.

When I stood, he playfully swatted my naked ass.

"Tucker," I pretended to scold him.

Still shirtless, he stretched his arms above his head. The movement caused his muscles to ripple. It took every ounce of restraint I had not to throw myself on top of him.

"See something you like?" His mouth turned up in a smirk.

"You're so damn cocky."

"You like it," he joked.

I licked my lips. Hell yeah, I liked it. I grabbed the shirt and shorts from earlier, slipped them back on, and gradually opened the bedroom door.

Shayne was still sound asleep, though I wasn't quite sure how she managed to stay on the couch, considering she was nearly upside down. Without making a peep, I half-ran on my tiptoes back to my room. When I walked in, Tucker had his shirt was on, and he was straightening the blankets.

Yep, I am definitely keeping him.

"She's asleep, but I'm pretty sure she's seconds away from falling off the couch."

He laughed. "She usually sleeps like that. The kid is a mess." He gave me a chaste kiss.

We exited the room, and I followed him into the kitchen. He eased the door open and made his getaway.

I took in the furniture arrangement on the back porch, and my cheeks heated as I remembered what we had done last night. I stepped out and began putting things back to rights, cleaning up the mess we'd been too preoccupied to attend to last night. When I was finished, I went back inside, closing the door behind me and walked over to the sink to wash my hands. After I dried them, I turned and came face-to-face with a wide-awake five-year old.

"Ahhh!" I screamed. "Shit. Shayne, you scared me to death."

Her eyes went large, and her mouth made a perfect O. Then, she asked, "Do you have a swear jar?"

"A what?"

"You know, a jar you put quarters in when you say bad words?"

"No."

"You should get one, and when you do, you owe the jar a quarter because you just said shit."

"Shayne!"

"What? That doesn't count. I was explaining how it works."

This kid.

Shayne looked around the room and then down at her clothes. "Did we have a sleepover?"

I had no idea how to answer her, but that sure sounded plausible, so I decided to go with it. "Um ... yes, we did."

"Where did Daddy sleep? Is he awake yet?"

Fuckity fuck.

The way I saw it, I had two choices. I could either lie or distract her.

The covered dish on the island caught my eye. "How about a cupcake?"

Her eyes lit up at the suggestion. "Yes, please."

I pulled out the stool, so she could climb onto it. Then, I poured her a glass of milk, gave her a cupcake, and started a pot of coffee. Maybe, if I kept busy, she wouldn't ask any more questions. If Tucker didn't hurry, then I'd probably just keep feeding her sweets for breakfast. It seemed like a completely rational plan. Fine, it wasn't rational at all, but whatever. If Shayne's mouth was full, she couldn't ask questions.

I silently willed Tucker to hurry up. As if summoned by the thought alone, the front door opened, and he walked through it.

27

TUCKER

I opened the door to Camryn's without knocking, uncertain if Shayne would be awake or not. I hadn't needed to worry. She was in the kitchen, shoving a cupcake into her mouth, so I dropped the bag containing her change of clothes on the couch and walked over to where she sat at the island.

"Good morning, Doodlebug." I tousled her hair and kissed the top of her forehead.

"Morning, Daddy." She smiled, and pink frosting showed between the cracks in her teeth. She took a drink of her milk and then asked, "Why did I sleep here? Did you have a sleepover, too?"

I looked to Camryn, who only shrugged. "Bug, how about we go out to breakfast?"

"I already ate breakfast," she said matter-of-factly.

"That," I said, pointing to the paper wrapper gripped in her hand, "is not breakfast."

"Okay. Can Camryn come with us?"

"Yes."

"Yay," she shrieked, dropping the now-empty liner.

"Camryn, do you like pancakes?" Before she had a chance to answer, Shayne directed her next question to me. "Can we go to Pancake Palace?"

I looked toward Camryn. "Does that work for you?"

"Sure," she said, grinning.

I imagined, she found this all very amusing. It didn't take long for the girls to get ready. We loaded up in my truck and drove into town, Shayne's chatter a constant in the background.

A few minutes after we arrived at Pancake Palace, we were seated in a booth. We placed our order, and when the waitress walked away, I turned my attention to Shayne. She sat across from me on the inside of the booth, next to Camryn.

"Bug, I want to talk to you about something."

"Am I in trouble? Because, whatever it is, I'm pretty sure I didn't do it," she said, elbows on the table, chin resting in her palms. She batted her lashes, exuding angelic innocence. Once she was a teenager, I'd be so screwed.

I laughed. "No, you aren't in trouble."

Just then, the server returned with a coffee for Camryn and me and a chocolate milk for Shayne. I nodded my thanks and waited for her to walk away.

Before I could say anything, Shayne asked, "Daddy, is Camryn your girlfriend?"

Camryn started choking on her sip of coffee. "Sorry. It just went down the wrong way."

"Are you all right?" Shayne patted Camryn's back.

"Yes, sweet girl. Thank you."

"You're welcome."

"Bug, Camryn is my girlfriend. That's what I wanted to talk to you about."

"Does that mean you guys are going to hold hands and kiss and stuff?" She crinkled her nose.

"Sometimes." I grinned.

"That's gross." Shayne shifted in her seat, looking at Camryn. "You're still my friend though, right?"

"Of course." Camryn tucked a wayward strand of hair behind Shayne's ear.

"Okay." She shrugged.

That was the extent of her reaction. I'd expected her to ask more questions. Something other than her being nonchalant about the whole thing. She was the kind of kid who mulled things over, so maybe the questions would come later.

"Daddy, breakfast is taking forever."

"Want to play tic-tac-toe?" Camryn asked Shayne while she rifled through her purse.

"Sure."

Camryn produced two pens from her purse and flipped over the paper placemat on the table. She drew the lines and let Shayne go first. Since they were caught up in their game, it gave me a chance to watch them, and the view made my heart ache in the best way. If that made me sound like a pussy, I didn't give a damn. For the first time in my life, this was what I wanted. Not out of a sense of obligation to do the right thing, but because I couldn't imagine my life without either one of my girls.

In my periphery, I saw the waitress approaching, balancing our breakfast on a large serving tray.

"All right, folks, who gets the steak and eggs?" she asked.

I raised an index finger.

Camryn cleared space before her and Shayne while the server set a Denver omelet with a side of fruit in front of Camryn.

"That must mean, this one is yours." She smiled and set the plate in front of Shayne.

Shayne's eyes grew wide, and a huge smile spread across her face as she took in the plate. She'd ordered something called a Unicorn Stack. Four small chocolate chip pancakes were assembled on top of each other. Each one was a different color, and on top sat a swirl of whipped cream that resembled a horn. Pink and purple sugar sprinkles finished off the plate. The kid would be on a sugar high for days.

"This is the best day of my life," Shayne declared.

Camryn turned to her and laughed. "Those look amazing."

The waitress refilled our coffee cups before asking, "Can I get you folks anything else?"

"Need anything, babe?" I asked Camryn.

"No, thank you. I think we're good."

"All right. Y'all enjoy, and I'll be back to check on you."

We ate quietly for a few minutes until I broke the silence, my eyes landing on Camryn. "What are your plans for tomorrow?"

"I don't really have any. Why?" she asked.

"I'd like you to come to Sunday supper." I waited for her reaction.

She stopped mid-chew, her eyes meeting mine, and then she swallowed hard and reached for her coffee.

Before I could say anything, Shayne interjected, "You have to come to Sunday supper." Then, she singsonged, "We can play on the tire swing, and Grammy makes the most amazing cookies."

"You want me to meet your mom?"

I heard the surprise in her voice. Camryn knew how important my mom was to me, and if she didn't know how serious I was about us already by disclosing our relationship to Shayne, she certainly knew it now.

"Yes." I reached across the table and gave her hand a gentle squeeze. "Relax. She'll love you." I released her and picked up my fork.

"All right. You sure she won't mind me just showing up?"

"I'm sure."

"Okay. Sunday supper it is."

"Yay," Shayne squealed.

We finished breakfast and drove back to the house. Camryn mentioned that she had plans tonight with Macy, and since Bug was spending the night with my mom, I thought about seeing if Nash wanted to grab a beer tonight after the shop closed.

After we piled out of the truck, Camryn hugged Shayne good-bye, and I walked her to her front door.

"You good?" I asked.

"More than good. Thank you for breakfast."

"Anytime, baby." I brushed my lips against hers, making sure to keep the kiss light. Shayne was busy playing on the grass, but I didn't want to get carried away. There would be time for that later.

"Are you coming over later tonight?" she asked.

"That depends. Do you want me to?" There was only one answer I wanted to hear. I gripped her hand in mine.

"Of course. I'll text you when I get home." She kissed me, and as we stepped away from each other, her fingers slipped from my grasp.

28

CAMRYN

I put the finishing touches on my makeup, slipped on a pair of strappy sandals, grabbed my purse, and headed out the door. Macy and I were meeting at The Hideaway for drinks and some long-overdue girl time.

During the drive to the bar, I thought about how everything was falling into place. I was in love with an incredible man, who had a little girl I adored. I loved my job, and after all this time, it finally felt like I wasn't alone anymore. That I could love without abandon. The knee-jerk reaction to protect myself from being hurt had faded.

A smile graced my lips as I parked the car and got out, making my way into the bar. The music hit my ears as I pulled the door open. Stepping inside, I scanned the crowd, and Macy's gorgeous mane of red hair wasn't hard to spot. She was sitting at one of the vinyl booths near the bar, and when her eyes landed on me, she raised her hand and waved. As I approached, she stood and pulled me into a quick hug.

"Camryn, it's so good to see you," she said, taking a seat.

"Sorry. I hope you weren't waiting long." I settled in beside her.

"Girl"—she stopped mid-sentence and took a sip of a fruity-looking cocktail from a mason jar—"don't even worry. I just got here about ten minutes ago." Her voice was slightly raised to be heard over the music.

"And you already have a drink." I laughed.

"Mack, the guy who owns the bar, is my dad's best friend, so he's more like a surrogate uncle. It's definitely a perk on nights like tonight." She waved a finger toward the crowd.

I nodded as I looked around for a server and saw one headed in our direction.

"Hey, y'all," she greeted us with a friendly smile.

"Kel, this is Camryn." Macy gestured her finger at me. "Camryn, this is Kelly, Mack's daughter."

"So, you're the new girl in town?" She smiled, her perfectly straight white teeth on display.

"Are they still calling me that?" I mean, I'd been here long enough to not be considered the new girl in town.

"They'll probably call you that until someone else moves to town," she joked. "What can I get for y'all?"

I ordered a Corona, and Macy ordered another strawberry-whiskey lemonade and some pretzel bites with beer-cheese sauce.

"So, tell me," Macy said and conspiratorially leaned in, "how's everything going with Tucker?"

My smile was wide, and I felt the heat rush to my cheeks.

"Damn, girl. That's what I'm talking about." She laughed. "Is the cat out of the bag?"

What she really wanted to know was if we'd told Shayne.

I nodded and said, "Tucker told Shayne this morning. We took her out for breakfast."

"Wow."

Just then, Kelly returned with our drinks and appetizer. We assured her we were fine, and she hurried away to attend to other patrons.

"I'm so happy for y'all. God knows, if anyone deserves to be happy, it's Tucker."

"He's amazing."

"They don't make 'em like that anymore; that's for damn sure." Macy dipped a pretzel into the cheese. "First, that bitch Holly ... then losing Dani and raising Shayne on his own ..." She popped the food into her mouth, swallowed it, and then picked up her glass.

"Holly?"

Who the hell is Holly?

A deer-in-the-headlights look crossed her face, and she set the drink back on the table with a thud. "He hasn't mentioned Holly?"

"No."

"It's not a big deal, and it was practically a hundred years ago," she exaggerated. "Let's just forget I said anything."

Unsure of what to say, I picked up my beer and drained it. I was a little bothered that Tucker hadn't shared that part of his past with me, but everybody had a past and obviously, Holly wasn't relevant. I set the empty bottle down on the table just as the jukebox started playing "Somewhere on a Beach" by Dierks Bentley.

"I love this song. Come on, girl. Let's go shake our moneymakers." She stood and pulled me from the booth.

"Moneymakers?" I busted out laughing. "Did you start drinking before you got here?"

"Oh, hush and move your ass." She playfully bumped her hip into mine.

We made our way to the small dance floor and began moving our bodies to the beat of the music. After we danced to several more songs, Macy and I returned to our table and ordered another round of drinks.

While we waited for Kelly to return with them, I asked, "What's the deal with you and Nash?"

"It's a long story." She hesitated before continuing, "We were high school sweethearts, and before I went off to college, we broke up. Things did not end well."

"That sucks."

"There's a lot of history between us, and the past can't be rewritten." A hint of sadness lurked in her eyes.

Kelly returned with our drinks and quickly left to wait on other customers.

"I'm sorry," I said and tipped the bottle to my lips, taking a long pull. All the dancing had made me a little sweaty, and ice-cold beer cooled me from the inside out.

"It is what it is, right? Besides, I hate him." She bent her head to capture the straw in her mouth and sucked down her drink.

The look on Macy's face and the tone of her voice told me she was lying.

"You know what they say ... there's a fine line between love and hate." I smiled innocently. "Drink faster, and let's get back out there."

We finished our drinks and hit the dance floor again, moving our bodies in time to the music, and I couldn't remember the last time I'd had so much fun.

"I'll be right back. I'm going to the ladies' room," Macy shouted over the music.

Since I didn't have to go, I continued to dance solo. Macy

had been gone mere seconds when a pair of hands gripped my waist from behind. Warm breath hit my neck, and it made my skin crawl. The stench of alcohol oozed from his pores, and I froze.

"Don't stop, baby," a male voice I didn't recognize growled in my ear. "We're just getting started." The stranger tightened his hold, fingers digging into my hips, his erection at my back.

"Let me go." All my senses came back to me, and I tried to struggle free.

The pressure of his grip increased. "Don't act like you don't want it. You're out here, shaking your ass, practically begging for it."

For a split second, I panicked until everything my dad had ever taught me came rushing back.

I can do this. He only has to think I want him.

I placed my hands on top of his and played along, reminding myself to keep my wits about me. It was working because his grip loosened just enough for me to turn to face him. He had a few inches on me, but he wasn't quite as tall as Tucker, and he was stocky. I flattened my palms on his chest, using my touch as a distraction. With my lip pulled between my teeth in a way that suggested I liked his hands on me, we moved in time to the music. His hands held fast to my waist, but I managed to create enough distance between us for what I had in mind.

I made a fist, pulled my arm back, and drove it forward, landing a hard punch to Mystery Man's nose. He stumbled back, his hands going to his face. Red seeped between the cracks of his fingers.

"Fucking bitch," he snarled.

Wiping the blood on his jeans, he lunged at me with his fist cocked, but before the stranger could do any harm, a different pair of arms yanked me out of the way, and I was pitched backward into a hard chest.

Chaos erupted around me.

"You fucking piece of shit." The sound was a thunderous roar.

Chairs scattered, glass shattered, and a table was upended.

I tried to struggle free of the arms wrapped around my torso.

"Easy there, slugger."

I recognized that voice. "Nash?" I asked, turning my head back to look at him.

Just then, Macy appeared beside us.

"What the hell, Cam? I left you alone for less than five min—"

"Macy, you two stay the hell back." Nash's words cut her off. "Do not let Camryn out of your sight," he demanded, half-shoving me at Macy before he lunged forward.

"Tucker! Come on, man, that's enough!" Panic surged through Nash's voice.

Mystery Man was on the ground, and Tucker was on top of him with his forearm across my aggressor's throat, putting enough pressure on his windpipe that Mystery Man's face was turning purple.

"Oh my God," I shrieked. "Tucker."

I took a step, but Macy grabbed my arm. "Camryn, don't."

I wrenched out of her grasp and went to Tucker's side.

My hand shook as I reached out to place it on his bicep. "Tucker, look at me." I waited for his eyes to lift to mine, and when they did, I said, "Tucker, it's okay. I'm fine."

His eyes roamed over my face before they moved down my body, searching for the truth. Finally convinced, he turned his attention back to the man beneath him. "Apologize to the lady," he seethed and removed the arm from his throat to allow him to breathe.

Mystery Man coughed and wheezed as he attempted to suck air into his lungs. He looked like he might tell Tucker to go to hell but seemed to think better of it. When he managed to suck in enough oxygen, he pinned me with a glare. "Sorry," he rasped out. Looking back at Tucker, he said, "Get the fuck off of me."

"You call that an apology? Try again, asshole," Tucker ordered.

Mystery Man's eyes were full of disdain when he twisted his neck to look at me. "I'm sorry, ma'am."

"Better." Tucker's voice was full of condescension. "When I let you up, you're going to go settle your tab and give Mack there a little extra for his troubles. Then, you're going to leave, and if I ever see you anywhere near her again, I will rain hell down on you like the fucking devil himself." Tucker stood and stepped over Mystery Man's body, pulling me into his side.

The crowd dispersed and went back to their business like nothing had happened. Without any further incident, the nameless man got up and walked to the bar.

"You okay, baby?" Tucker held me at arm's length while his eyes traveled over my body.

"I'm fine."

He drew me into him.

"What are you doing here anyway?" I asked.

"I was going to grab a beer with Nash."

I turned my head and saw Nash tipping the table back into its upright position. Then, he and Macy replaced the chairs around it. Kelly and one of her coworkers had a broom and dustpan in hand to sweep up the broken glass.

"Camryn, are you all right?" Worry filled Macy's eyes as she looked me over.

"I'm fine." I supported my right hand in my left palm. The burst of adrenaline had subsided, and it hurt like a bitch.

Tucker took my injured hand, gently cradling it in his. "Come on, you need to get some ice on that." He led me to the bar with Nash and Macy on our heels.

A man, whom I assumed was Mack, stood behind the bar. He appeared to be in his late fifties with graying hair and kind eyes. He shook his head as he headed in our direction. Coming to a stop in front of us, he opened his mouth to speak.

"Uncle Mack," Macy cut him off before Mack had the chance to get words out. "Can we get some ice for Rocky?" She jutted her thumb my way.

"Very funny." I rolled my eyes at her and then turned to Mack. "I'm sorry about that."

"Young lady, don't apologize. That son of a bitch had it coming. I was coming out from the bar with my bat, but Tucker made it there before I did. Let's get that hand taken care of." Mack went to put some ice in a clean bar mop towel and then brought it back to me.

"Thanks," I said as I took it from him. I gingerly placed the wrapped ice on top of my swollen knuckles, wincing at the contact.

Mack pinned Tucker and Nash with a glare. "If you boys are done disturbing the peace, maybe you ought to order a drink."

"I'm good," Tucker said while he reached into his back pocket for his wallet. He took out several bills and placed them on the bar. "Sorry for the disruption, Mack." Tucker turned to Macy. "Mace, do you mind giving Nash a ride back to his place? I'm going to take Camryn home."

"What about my car?" I asked.

I'd only had two beers, and we'd danced our asses off, so I wasn't drunk by a long shot. Macy had had more to drink than I did.

Nash spoke up, "Are you blind, man? Macy is half-lit."

"I am not." She sounded indignant.

Nash turned to Macy. "Give me your keys."

"No," she argued.

"Knock it off, all of you." Mack's firm tone caught our attention. "Macy, give Nash your keys. You aren't driving."

"Uncle Mack—"

"You heard me," he cut her off and then turned to me. "Rocky, go with Tucker. You can pick up your car tomorrow. It will be fine here overnight."

"Great. Since that's settled, Camryn and I are out," Tucker said, and his hand went to the small of my back.

Reluctantly, Macy gave Nash her keys before she came over to give me a hug, careful to avoid my injury.

"I'm sorry," I whispered in her ear.

"Don't even worry about it. Next time, maybe we should go out for coffee instead." She laughed.

"Sounds like a plan."

The four of us walked out of the bar together. Nash and Macy headed in one direction, and Tucker and I went in the other.

We got into his truck and barely spoke on the way home. As we approached my front door, I awkwardly dug in my purse for my keys. My fingers wrapped around them, and I fumbled as I inserted a key into the lock.

"Here, let me," Tucker said as he took the keys and

unlocked the door. Then, he stepped inside and flipped on the light.

"You were pretty quiet on the way home," I stated as I closed the door behind me.

"I was standing at the bar with Nash, waiting to order a drink, when I turned around and saw you with that asshole." He tossed my keys on the coffee table and went into the kitchen.

"Tucker," I called out, following behind him.

He opened the refrigerator, grabbed a beer, twisted off the cap, and took a slow pull.

"Look, I'm sure, from where you were standing, it probably looked bad for half a second."

He set his beer down on the island and stepped closer. "It was the longest half-second of my life, Camryn, but I knew something was off by your body language. By the time I made it over to you, your fist was connecting with his nose." He lifted my bruised knuckles to his lips and gently kissed them. "Remind me never to piss you off."

"Tucker, I love you. I would never—"

He pressed his mouth to mine, effectively silencing my words.

"Come on, Rocky. Let's go to bed."

I grabbed his beer from the island and let him lead me to my bedroom.

29

CAMRYN

I cracked my eyes open, blinking against the sunlight pouring in through the blinds covering the window. A groan left my lips as I stretched my limbs. With his warm palm splayed across my stomach, Tucker pulled me closer, and I snuggled into him.

"Good morning, beautiful." The timbre of his voice slid over me. Gravelly and thick with sleep, it was sexy as hell.

"Morning." I turned my head, and he bent to meet my lips in a chaste kiss. "What time is it?"

"Not sure."

"What time do we need to be at your mom's?"

"Not for a while."

We quietly lay there for several minutes, my back to his front. Tucker grazed the tips of his fingers back and forth across my belly. My sore hand brought me back to the memory of last night and the chat I'd had with Macy before it all went south. When I was facing away from Tucker, it was easier to work up my nerve to ask him the one question that I couldn't get out of my mind. I had planned to leave well enough alone, but in the light of day, I needed answers to the questions running around in my head on an endless loop.

"Tucker?"

"Hmm?"

"Who's Holly?"

His entire body tensed, and his fingers stopped moving.

"Macy mentioned her last night ..." I trailed off.

"Did she now? Tell me, what did Macy have to say?"

"Nothing. When Macy realized I had no clue whom she was talking about, she refused to elaborate."

He exhaled, and I felt him relax the tiniest bit.

"So, who is she?" I pressed. I wasn't jealous, just curious.

"Nobody." There was an edge to his tone.

"Really?"

Everything about his reaction told a different story.

"She's just an ex."

No way in hell is she just an ex.

"Before Dani or after?"

The mattress shifted as he sat up. I rolled over in time to see him planting his feet on the floor.

He cocked his head over his shoulder to look back at me. "I told you before, there hasn't been anyone since Dani until you. Holly," he spat her name like a curse, "is irrelevant."

He got out of bed, and the sight of his naked torso made my breath hitch.

"Tucker, wait." I rose up onto my knees, and the sheet fell away, exposing my bare frame.

His eyes made a slow perusal over my body before they locked on mine.

Tucker's entire demeanor had changed when I mentioned her name. Whoever the bitch was, she had obviously done a number on him, and I wanted my carefree man back, so I held out my hand to him.

"I'm sorry. I was just curious. I didn't mean to upset you."

He took my outstretched hand and gently tugged me closer. His arm went around my back as he brushed away the hair that had fallen across my face. "The past needs to stay where it is."

"Okay," I agreed, letting it go.

All the tension left his body. He leaned in, pressed his mouth to mine, and sucked my bottom lip between his teeth. Heat flared between my legs as he deepened the kiss.

His stomach picked that moment to growl loud enough that it nearly echoed through the quiet space. A low chuckle left his lips. "Guess I'm hungry."

"Want me to whip something up? I can make omelets or maybe French toast, but I'm not sure if I have bread."

"Camryn."

"What?"

Those stunning hazel eyes pierced mine. "Forget about food. The only thing I want to eat is right here in front of me."

Yes, please. My cheeks heated.

"Lie back." His mellow tone made it seem like a request, but given the look on his face, it was the furthest thing from it.

As long as he kept looking at me like that, I'd do just about anything. My back met the pillowy softness of the mattress.

With his weight supported by his arms, Tucker hovered over me. Our gazes connected.

"Love you, baby." He dipped his head, and starting at my neck, he trailed warm kisses over my skin.

Goose bumps danced over my flesh as my body reacted to his touch.

"I love you, too," I said, my voice breathy.

He moved lower, inching his way down my torso, stoking the fire burning inside me.

~

After we spent the morning in bed, we took a shower, had a light breakfast, and ran to pick up my car from The Hideaway. We dropped it back off before we headed to his mom's house for Sunday supper later that afternoon.

I stared out the truck window, incessantly bouncing my leg. Music drifted through the speakers, but it did little to take my mind off the horrible case of nerves I was suffering from.

Tucker sensed my unease, and his right hand shifted from the steering wheel to my jumping appendage. "Cam, stop. She's going to love you."

"How can you be so sure?" I asked.

"Because it's impossible not to love you." He spoke the words like a man who'd fought the battle and lost.

He was so sweet, but it didn't change the fact that I was still anxious about meeting his mom even though he'd told me a hundred times that I didn't have anything to worry about. Jared's mom had hated me simply because she never thought I was good enough for her baby boy. The truth was, I wasn't great with moms, and I was sure it stemmed from the fact that I didn't have one. I took a deep, calming breath.

We drove up the long gravel driveway and came to a stop outside a beautiful, modest farmhouse with a huge porch. It was the kind of house you looked at and somehow knew that love lived and breathed within its walls.

I'd barely made it out of the truck when Shayne was at my side.

"Camryn, you came."

She threw herself into my arms, and I picked her up, squeezing tightly, wincing slightly at my still-tender hand.

"Hey, sweet girl. Did you have fun with Grammy?"

"Yes."

"I see how it is, Bug. You're so excited to see Camryn, you forget all about Daddy," Tucker teased.

"Aw, poor Daddy. Maybe you should go give him some love," I said and released her.

Tucker opened his arms, and Shayne ran to him.

"Daddy, I could never forget about you." She wrapped her arms around his neck.

We walked up the stairs that led to the porch where Tucker's mom was waiting for us.

"Hi, Mom." Tucker reached for her with his free arm and drew her into a hug. A long second later, Tucker freed her and set Shayne on her feet.

Shayne made a beeline for the porch swing while Tucker introduced me to his mom, "Mom, this is Camryn. Cam, this is my mom, Laura."

Her arms embraced me. "Camryn, I am so happy to meet you."

I heard the truth in her words, and a sense of relief washed over me as I returned her affection.

"Easy, Mom."

Laura stepped back and playfully smacked Tucker on the arm. "Hush, you. I hope y'all are hungry. Come on inside."

She opened the screen door, and we all filed into the house behind her.

"You good, baby?" Tucker asked, leaning in close, his hand on the small of my back.

"I'm great." I looked up at him and smiled.

Shayne got in the middle and took each of our hands,

tugging us toward the kitchen. "I helped Grammy make Rice Krispies Treats, and they're super yummy."

I laughed and knew exactly what she was up to.

Obviously, so did Tucker because he said, "Nice try, Bug. Let's wash up, and we'll help Grammy set the table."

"Oh, man. Okay."

The three of us walked over to the sink and took turns in washing our hands. Tucker and Shayne went to set the table on the back deck, leaving Laura and me in the house together.

"What can I do to help?"

"There's homemade strawberry lemonade in a pitcher on the top shelf of the fridge, if you don't mind grabbing it. There's a stack of Solo cups in the cabinet to the left of the icebox, too. We'll just take everything outside."

"Sure." I did as she'd asked and carried everything out to the table.

"I'm going to help Mom carry out the food. I'll be right back." Tucker kissed the top of my head and walked back inside.

Seconds later, arms laden with food, Tucker and Laura appeared. Shayne was already in her chair, waiting patiently. Tucker placed a platter of pot roast on the table. Laura set mashed potatoes and green beans alongside it.

"All right, I'm going to grab the gravy boat and the rolls. Do we need anything else?" Laura asked.

"I think we're good, Mom," Tucker said.

I poured lemonade into each of the cups and sat next to Shayne. Tucker waited for his mom to return, and once she emptied her hands, he pulled her chair out for her before he took his seat.

"Please help yourselves," Laura said.

I picked up Shayne's plate and held it, so Tucker could

place roast on it. Then, I added a spoonful of the veggies and set it in front of her.

"Do you want gravy, kiddo?" I asked her.

"Yes, please."

"Here you go." Laura passed me the gravy boat with a megawatt smile on her face, and I put a spoonful over Shayne's mashed potatoes.

The rest of us made our plates and began to eat. The dinner conversation was light, and we laughed and joked. I was hit with the realization that this was what I wanted more than anything in the world. To be part of a family—not just any family, but *their* family. All at once, I felt overcome with emotion, and I excused myself to the bathroom.

"It's down the hall, second door on the left," Laura said.

"Thank you. I'll be right back." I got up and went inside.

As I made my way through the house, I noticed the pictures scattered throughout the living room and in the hallway. One in particular caught my eye, and I stepped closer to inspect it. Younger versions of Tucker, Nash, and Macy stared back at me. I recognized Dani from the picture that I had seen on Tucker's fridge months ago, though she looked much healthier in this photo. I didn't have to guess who the gorgeous blonde was flanking Tucker's other side. Judging by the way they looked at each other, they were completely enamored. The remaining guy in the snapshot could've been Tucker's twin. They had the same eyes and very similar smiles. I stared at the photograph, fully aware there were parts of Tucker's life I knew nothing about.

"I can't bring myself to take that picture down. They were all so happy back then. Had their whole lives ahead of them," Laura said quietly.

I jumped at the sound of her voice and pressed a hand over my heart.

"I'm sorry. I didn't mean to scare you."

"No, it's fine. You surprised me; that's all." I was quiet for a second and then asked, "Is that ... I mean, does Tucker have a brother?"

"Griffin, my oldest." She nodded and stretched her index finger forward, pressing it to the glass. "He's been gone for six years. The boys weren't quite a year apart."

"Tucker never talks about him." I hadn't even been aware he had a brother until now.

"I know." Those two words were weighted with so much sadness. "Even after all this time, it's so hard for him. They were best friends their whole lives. They were nearly inseparable until Griffin joined the military. When we lost Griff ... Tuck never had time to grieve. He was too busy holding everyone else together. I still don't think he's grieved. Not really."

"I had no idea." My heart ached for her and for Tucker, too.

I had grown up as an only child. I had no idea what it was like to have a sibling, let alone lose one, and I couldn't imagine losing a child. Shayne wasn't mine, but just the thought of losing her made me physically ill. It was unfathomable.

I turned to Laura and said the same words I'd grown to hate because I'd heard them so many times, "I'm so sorry for your loss." I meant every syllable to my core.

She reached over, took my hand, and gave it a squeeze before dropping it. "Thank you."

I already knew the answer, but I had to ask anyway, "The blonde beside Tucker ... who is she?"

"Holly." Her tone was laced with dejection and contempt.

Obviously, Holly had hurt Tucker deeply, but he'd had a

baby with Dani, so maybe he'd been the one to hurt Holly. Though, from his reaction this morning, I didn't think that was the case. It didn't feel right to press Tucker's mom for more information.

Laura seemed lost in her memories, and I wanted to give her a little space, so I took a step toward the bathroom even though I didn't really have to go.

"Camryn ..."

I stopped and turned back to face her. "Yes?"

She protectively folded her arms over her chest. "He loves you."

"I know."

"Do you though?"

Her question caught me a little off guard, and I quizzically looked at her. "I think so."

"He's never let anyone get close ... not since ..." She blew out a hard breath and gave a slight shake of her head, as if she knew perhaps some things were better left alone. "Please don't hurt him."

The look on her face nearly cracked me in two.

"I love your son. More than I ever thought possible. And I love your granddaughter, too. As long as they'll have me, I'm not going anywhere."

She crossed the space between us and wrapped me in a hug. "Welcome to the family." She held me for a few long seconds, and when she pulled away, she said, "Now, how about we grab ourselves some Rice Krispies Treats, and you can tell me all about how you got that bruise on your hand. It looks pretty badass, and I'm thinking there is a story there."

I laughed hard because I realized my being anxious to meet Laura Jaxson was the most ridiculous thing in the world.

30

TUCKER

A few weeks had passed since Camryn first joined us for Sunday supper at my mom's. Since then, she and my mom had hung out a few times. Once, they'd even taken Shayne out together for a girls' day, and I loved that the three of them were spending time together.

Every day, I fell more in love with Camryn. She was the piece I hadn't known was missing, and I wanted to make her a permanent part of our family. Nothing had ever felt so right. Maybe it was too soon, and there were logistics that had to be worked out. There was a part of my past she didn't know about, but in the grand scheme of things, it didn't matter because it didn't change the truth. And the truth was, I wanted her, and I wanted a life with us.

For the last several years, it'd felt like I was going through the motions. Camryn had changed everything for me, and if I wanted a future with her, I had to fully let go of the past.

It was the Thursday before Thanksgiving. Things at work were a little slow, and since I had some time before I needed to leave to get Shayne from school, I went into my office and closed the door, not wanting to take the chance of anyone overhearing my conversation.

I pulled up the contact in my phone and pressed the Call icon.

"This is Darius."

Darius Cannon was the owner of Cannon Custom Homes.

"Hey, man, it's Tucker Jaxson."

"Tucker, it's been a while. How's everything going?"

"Good. Better than good actually. Listen"—I kicked my feet up on my desk and leaned back in my chair—"I was wondering, how soon would it be possible to break ground?"

"Are you messing with me, Jaxson? You've been sitting on that land forever."

He had a point.

"Nope. It's time."

"Let me check on a few things real quick." Papers rustled in the background. Darius was silent for several beats. "We're probably looking at March."

I still had to have the land cleared. "That sounds perfect."

We talked for a little more, and Darius gave me the names of a few land-clearing operators, which I jotted down on a piece of paper. After I hung up with him, I told Nash I was heading out. There was something I wanted to take care of, and I didn't want to give myself a chance to back out.

I drove home and grabbed what I needed from my closet. If I hurried, I'd have enough time to drop the plans off at the blueprint shop for them to make a copy. My only hope was that, in a few weeks, when Camryn got her Christmas gift, she'd be as excited as I was.

31

CAMRYN

Tucker came up behind me as I stood at the kitchen island, chopping onions and celery for the dressing. His warm lips ghosted across the sensitive spot where my neck and shoulder met.

"Do you have any idea how fucking sexy you are in that apron?" he whispered against the shell of my ear.

"Tucker, if you keep it up, I'm never going to get everything done for tomorrow," I protested.

We were spending Thanksgiving with Laura, and I'd offered to help her with the meal prep. Since school was out, Tucker let Shayne spend the night at her grammy's, and instead of relishing the alone time, my mood was melancholic. Normally, I loved his touch. The man could probably achieve world peace by his mouth alone, but today, I was struggling, and my emotions were overriding my libido.

I gathered the veggies into the bowl I had at the ready and skirted around Tucker to get to the stove. After I turned the burner on under the skillet I already had waiting, I grabbed the sage sausage from the fridge, opened it, and then added it to the pan along with the onions and celery.

Heat bloomed at my back, and I didn't have to turn around to know Tucker was watching me. I needed a minute to gather myself without the scrutiny of his gaze.

"Do you mind watching this for a minute? I need to go to the bathroom," I asked without facing him.

"Sure," he said.

When I went to walk past him, he reached out for me. He gently tugged me closer. Hooking his finger, he slid it under my chin and angled my face to meet his eyes.

"What's wrong, baby? You seem a little off."

"I just need a minute," I said, not really looking at him.

He must have seen something in my eyes because he didn't push. "Okay."

He dropped his hand, and I made my exit.

Once in the bathroom, I closed the door behind me and sat down on the closed toilet lid. Tomorrow would be the first major holiday without my dad, and I missed him so much, there was a soul-deep ache in my chest. Sorrow gripped my heart as I thought of the man who'd been both mom and dad for me. I missed the earthy way he'd smelled. A mix of grease, dirt, sweat, and the lingering scent of Brut. I missed the way he'd argue with the television and how he'd make such a damn production of carving the turkey every single year.

Slow, fat tears started as a trickle but quickly became a torrent. A sob escaped my throat, and I scrambled to turn on the faucet to drown out the sounds of my sadness. Then, I slunk to the bathroom floor, pulled my knees into my chest, buried my face in the crook of my arms, and bawled.

After several long minutes, I got up and washed my face. Then, I patted it dry and shut off the water. I drew a few calming breaths and caught my reflection in the mirror. Through red-rimmed eyes, I took in my splotchy cheekbones and groaned. There was no way Tucker wouldn't notice, but if I stayed in here much longer, I was certain he'd end up pounding on the door until I let him in.

When I was back in the kitchen, Tucker was bent over, loading dishes in the dishwasher. I headed to the stove and saw he had turned off the burner beneath the cooked sausage mixture, so I grabbed the pan and a trivet from the drawer and took them over to the island top.

"What's up?" he asked, taking a seat on one of the barstools.

"Nothing." The lie fell easily from my lips as I avoided his gaze, not wanting him to see how hard I'd been crying, and I got to work on finishing the dressing.

"You've been crying."

That hadn't taken long.

"Nothing really. Just a rough day."

He stood up and went to the fridge for a beer. He twisted off the cap and took a drink. Arms crossed, he leaned back against the counter, eyeing me.

"What?"

"Obviously, something is wrong."

"I told you … it's been a rough day. Besides, it's not like you talk to me about everything."

When I'd brought up Holly weeks ago, he'd shut me down. The conversation I'd had with his mom in the hallway left me with so many questions. I'd drawn the conclusion that Dani might have been his wife, and her death had made him a widower, but Holly was the woman who had broken him. He didn't talk about his dad or Griffin either.

"What do you want to know?" It might have been a question, but it was laced with a warning.

"How come you never told me you have a brother?" My tone wasn't accusatory or full of judgment.

"Had," he corrected, his pain nearly palpable. "I had a brother."

"Your mom said you were best friends."

"We were. There's nothing I wouldn't have done for him."

"Does it ever get easier?" My voice trembled. "The whole grieving thing, I mean." My watery gaze met his eyes.

"Shit," he said quietly.

And I knew he understood. Instantly, he was at my side, removing the spoon covered in saturated bread-crumbs from my hand and setting it down. He hauled me against his body, one arm around my waist while the other stroked my hair. "It's your first Thanksgiving without your dad."

A fresh wave of anguish slammed into me as his words hit my ears, and my body shook with silent sobs.

"I'm so sorry, baby," he said, comforting me. Gently, he began to sway our bodies ever so slightly.

The harder I cried, the tighter he held on.

"It's all right, Cam. Just breathe."

After what seemed like an eternity, I was able to reel in the onslaught of emotions and peeled my cheek from his soaked shirt.

"I'm sorry." I dried my face with the backs of my hands.

"Don't be, baby. That's what I'm here for." He tilted my chin up, forcing my eyes to his. "If you're sad or pissed or hurt, you talk to me."

I nodded, and Tucker softly brushed his lips against mine.

"It might make me sound like a selfish ass because I know how much you miss your dad"—he cupped my cheeks—"but I'm so fucking thankful you're standing here, in my arms."

His words hit me straight in the heart, and I swore, I could've melted into a puddle at his feet.

Tucker kissed me again, deeper this time. When he pulled away, he pressed his forehead to mine. "I love you."

"I love you, too."

He hugged me to him and asked, "What do you have left to make?"

"Cucumber salad and banana pudding." The words were muffled against his hard chest.

"How about we knock it out together, and you can tell me about your dad?"

"Are you sure you want to help?" I took a step back to look at him and placed my hands on my hips.

"I'm not going to just sit on my ass while you do all the work. Besides, I know my way around a kitchen." He attempted a wounded look. "Now, just tell me where I can get one of those things." He waved a finger over my apron.

I pointed him to the alcove where several hung on a hook, and then I walked to the sink to wash up.

"Damn. You think you have enough of these?"

I dried my hands and turned to see him rifling through the selection. "You can blame my Nonna for that obsession."

Tucker found the only manly-looking one I owned and slipped it over his head.

"Good choice," I said and pointed to his chest. It was black and had a rooster on the front with the word *cocky* embroidered in red above it. "It made me laugh, so I bought it."

"I can see why." He chuckled.

While Tucker washed his hands, I quickly finished spooning the dressing into the disposable pan. I covered it and put it in the fridge. Then, I grabbed the sour cream to start on the next item on my list.

"Can you grab another cutting board from that cabinet over there?" I asked, pointing to the one I was referring to. I rinsed the cucumbers and lightly ran the fresh dill under water. Then, I patted everything dry and took the ingredients to the island top.

He set the board down and shifted the stools out of the way. We worked quietly for a few minutes. Tucker thinly sliced the cucumbers while I chopped the dill and combined it in a bowl with the sour cream.

With the edge of his knife, he slid the slices from the cutting board into the bowl. "Tell me about him."

"Whenever I was sad, he'd try to make me laugh or do something special to cheer me up." I laughed as the memories began to flood back in. "I remember this one Halloween. I had my costume all set, and I was so excited to go trick-or-treating." I pressed the lid over the bowl of the creamy salad, stuck it in the fridge, and grabbed the milk for the banana pudding. "I ended up catching the stomach flu and couldn't go."

"That had to suck," he sympathized.

"It did." I got the pudding started, turned the fire to low, and stood sideways, so I could stir it and look at Tucker. "Oh, can you grab the vanilla wafers and layer them on the bottom of that pan?"

He opened the box of cookies to do as I'd asked.

"Anyway, I was devastated to have missed out on trick-or-treating. Two days later, when I was fully recovered, Dad made me put on my costume—"

"What did you dress up as?" he interrupted.

"Mother Goose." I snickered, remembering the getup. "Nonna had made the dress with a little white half-apron." I grinned. "Then, she'd printed out a few nursery rhymes on iron-on transfer paper, put them on it, and hot-glued a spider and a cow to the fabric. I had a giant floppy hat that tied under my chin and fake glasses, too. I was so damn adorable."

Tucker roared with laughter. "Please tell me there are pictures."

I stuck my tongue out at him. "Where was I?" I thought for a second, "Oh ... he made me put on the costume. When I asked him why, he said he was taking me trick-or-treating. I thought he was crazy, but I grabbed my pillow-case, and we went to every house on our street. When I knocked on the door and said those magic words, I ended up with tons of candy. The weird thing was, they were all my favorites." I smiled wistfully. "Years later, he confessed to buying all the sweets and getting the neighbors on board."

"He sounds like an incredible man."

"He really was."

We finished with the banana pudding and let it cool on the counter. While I threw together a quick antipasto salad for dinner, Tucker surprised me by sharing stories from his own childhood. With every laugh we shared, I felt the sadness ebb away.

After we ate dinner, put away all the food, and cleaned up the kitchen, we curled up on the couch to watch television.

When it cut to a commercial break, I slid from beneath Tucker's arms. "I'll be right back. There's something I want to show you."

I went to my bedroom and retrieved the box from the closet. I lifted out the folded material and hugged it to my chest as I headed back to the living room.

"Will you help me unfold this?" I asked upon my approach.

He stood, and I offered him an end of the fabric. Together, we opened the large white sheet.

The corner of his mouth tugged upward. "Are those turkeys?"

"Yep."

Dozens of turkeys, made from my and my dad's handprints through the years, decorated the material.

"Every Thanksgiving, after we ate breakfast, we'd paint our hands and add new turkeys. By the time we ate, the paint would be dry, and my dad would fold the sheet like a runner and put it on the table." I pointed to the littlest handprint near the corner Tucker was holding. "That's the first one. I was only three."

His smile was huge.

"What?" I asked, suddenly feeling self-conscious.

"I don't think you could be any more fucking adorable if you tried."

"That's it. No more show-and-tell for you," I joked.

Together, we refolded it, and after, I set it on the chair. Tucker pulled me in for hug, and I let out a yawn.

"Tired, baby?"

"A little."

"Why don't you go to bed? I'll be right there. I'm just going to call Mom and check on Bug."

"Okay," I said sleepily and headed down the hall.

32

TUCKER

I stepped out onto Camryn's back porch and dialed my mom's number.

She picked up on the second ring. "Tuck. You're calling a little late. Is everything okay?"

"Sorry, Mom. Everything is fine. I have a question for you."

Seeing my girl so lost in her grief had gutted me. I wanted to do something for her, and as soon as she'd brought out the sheet with all those little turkeys made from handprints, it'd hit me.

"All right."

"Remember all those paints you bought when you and Bug made those shirts? Do you still have them?"

"Yeah. Why?"

After I filled her in on my idea, she was quiet for several long seconds. I pulled the phone away from my ear to make sure she was still there.

"Mom?"

"I'm here," she sighed. She was trying to find her words,

so I waited. Finally, she said, "You're the best kind of man, Tucker Jaxson."

"You're biased."

"Maybe I am, but if ever there was anyone who deserved to be happy, it's you."

"I appreciate that, Mom."

A beat went by, and I braced myself for the question I knew was coming.

"Have you told her?"

"Not yet." I had my reasons, none of which I wanted to discuss with my mother.

"A lie of omission is still a lie, young man."

"Mom," I warned.

"Fine. I won't say another word, but at some point, you need to tell her."

I knew she was right, but doing that would require slashing open old wounds, ripping through scar tissue, and unleashing the truth I wanted to keep buried forever.

It was time for a change of subject. "How's Bug?"

"Good. Sound asleep. We played hard."

"Sounds like you wore her out."

"More like the other way around." She laughed. "I'm beat."

"In that case, I'll let you go. Thanks, Mom ... for everything. We'll see you tomorrow."

"Love you, Tuck."

"Love you, too."

There was no trace of sadness in my woman's eyes this morning when I found her in the kitchen, making cinnamon rolls.

I hoped today wouldn't be too hard on her, but I knew better than most that, sometimes, grief came in waves, knocking you down when you least expected it. Other times, you wouldn't need to look at a calendar because certain dates were branded into the recesses of your brain. You knew it was coming, and somehow, even though you mentally prepared, the pain was a fucking rip current sucking you below the surface.

Mom had called me earlier to say she had everything set up for our little project. I couldn't wait to surprise Camryn, and Shayne would love it, too.

We loaded up the truck and headed out. I watched Camryn out of my periphery as she sang along with the radio. Her long black hair was in a braid down her back. Blue-and-gray-checkered flannel with the sleeves rolled up to her elbows, several buttons undone, and the ends tied at the waist. Perfect amount of cleavage peeking out from the black tank she wore beneath her shirt. Legs clad in tight blue denim. She looked fuckable, and I debated on taking a detour down one of the back roads to do just that.

"Tucker?" she said my name like a question.

My eyes drifted from the road to look at her. "Yeah, baby?"

I glanced back to the windshield, slowed down, and made my turn onto the country road that led to my mom's. I shifted my gaze to her again, and I needed my mouth on her. To taste her in a way I wouldn't be able to for hours unless we somehow managed to get away from prying eyes. I looked in the rearview, made sure the coast was clear, and pulled the truck over onto the side of the road.

She gaped at me. "What are you doing?"

"This." I unbuckled my seat belt and then did the same to hers.

I hauled her closer. Gripping her braid, I wove it around my fist and brought my mouth to hers. My tongue glided along the seam of her lips. She opened, and I dipped inside, tasting the hint of sweet cinnamon. Camryn's hands went to my neck, and her fingers tugged at my hair. I loved the way her body reacted to mine. I wanted to devour her. Feast on every inch of her skin and have her again for dessert. I kissed her until my body's demand for oxygen could no longer be ignored.

With our foreheads together, we shared the same air as we panted for breaths.

"Holy shit," she gasped.

I chuckled.

"What was that for?" She pulled back to look at me.

"I couldn't go another minute without kissing you."

"Aw." She cupped my face. "Has anyone ever told you, you're the sweetest and sexiest man alive?"

"All the time." I smirked.

She playfully swatted me on the chest. "You're such a shit." She laughed.

"You love me," I countered.

She grew serious, moved her mouth to mine, and placed the barest whisper of a kiss against my lips. Then, she wrapped her arms around my neck, tightly squeezed, and said, "More than you'll ever know."

We sat there, embracing each other, for long moments. A sense of foreboding settled over me, and I didn't want to let her go.

"Your mom is going to start to wonder where we are," Camryn finally uttered.

I knew she was right, and as much as I didn't want to, I released my hold and shifted my body to put my seat belt back on as Camryn did the same. I pulled back out onto the road, and in a matter of minutes, we were in my mom's driveway.

"We're here," I called out as Camryn and I walked through the front door, arms weighted down with food.

"In here," Shayne and Mom called out in unison.

We followed their voices into the kitchen and began unloading everything.

"Daddy." Shayne threw herself into my now-free arms.

I picked her up and held her to me.

She hugged me tight and whispered into my ear, "Is it time for Camryn's surprise yet?"

"In just a few minutes. Keep it a secret a little longer," I whispered back.

"Okay." She looked into my eyes. "Did you miss me?"

"Always, Doodlebug."

"I love you, Daddy."

"I love you, too. How about you hop down, so I can help Grammy really quick?"

"Okay."

I set her on her feet and watched as she went to hug Camryn.

Several minutes later, after the dressing was in the oven and the turkey was taken out to rest, we all headed to the back porch where my mom had everything set up.

Newspaper covered the table as well as several small bottles of fabric paint, placemat-sized pieces of burlap, and everything else we would need.

"What's all this?" Camryn asked.

I put my arms around her and hugged her from behind. "I thought you could use some placemats to go with your table-runner thing."

"Tucker, I don't even know what to say." Her eyes moved to my mom. "Laura ..."

My girl was at a loss for words, and that didn't happen often.

"It was all Tucker. I just happened to have what he needed on hand."

The look on Camryn's face was priceless.

"This is incredible," Camryn said, taking it in. "Thank you."

"I've been waiting all day for this," Shayne announced. "Grammy said I had to be patient, and I tried so hard that I used all my patience up. Will you show me how to make a turkey now?" She looked at Camryn and gave her *that* face, complete with fluttering eyelashes and a pouty bottom lip. It worked like a charm every time.

Camryn took my daughter by the hand and sat at the table. My mom followed suit, and I watched the three people I loved more than anything in the world cover their palms in brown and then each finger in a different shade of paint.

I breathed deeply, taking it all in. My heart swelled at the sight before me, and I wanted to freeze time. The sounds of their combined laughter washed over me. I sat on the other side of my daughter and picked up a paintbrush. Camryn's eyes found mine, and in their depths, I swore, I could see forever.

I tried like hell to ignore it, but the uneasiness from earlier settled back in. No matter how hard I fought it, I couldn't shake the feeling that my life was about to implode.

33

CAMRYN

Nearly the last three weeks had flown by in a whirl of activity. Christmas was just shy of two weeks away, and winter break started today. I'd been spending as much time with Shayne and Tucker as possible. We had gone to the park and taken Shayne ice-skating at the faux rink the town of Jaxson Cove set up every winter. I loved them both with every bit of my soul.

I was on my way to the garage to pick up Shayne, so I could take her shopping for her dad's Christmas gift. Then, we were going to make gingerbread houses while Tucker worked late. I pulled into the lot and parked next to Tucker's truck. I got out of the car and smiled at the predictable chime of the door when I walked inside.

The lobby was empty, except for Nash, who was sitting behind the high counter.

"Hey, Camryn," he said louder than necessary.

"Hi, Nash."

"Camryn!" Shayne squealed in delight. A flurry of brown hair bounded around the corner of the counter. "Is it time to go shopping now?" She threw her arms around my waist and glanced up at me.

"In a few minutes, sweet girl. Where's your dad?"

"He's in there, talking to his friend." She pointed at Tucker's closed office door.

"Oh." The second my eyes landed on Nash, he looked away. "Nash, what's going on?"

"Camryn." He slightly shook his head.

What the hell?

I walked toward Tucker's office door but stopped short when Nash spoke, "Hold up a sec."

I pivoted to face him, and he pointed a finger at Shayne.

"Come on, Monkey," he said to Shayne. "Let's go see Aunt Macy."

"But Camryn is taking me shopping." She put her hands on her hips.

"We'll be right back. Besides, Aunt Macy has those little mints you love," he persuaded. "The square ones."

"Those ones are dinner mints."

"And they're your favorite. Come on. I'll even sneak you some for later."

Her eyes lit up. "Great idea. Camryn, don't leave without me."

"Not a chance, kiddo."

I waited until they left, knocked once on Tucker's office door, and twisted the knob.

Tucker was leaning against the short end of his desk while a woman with long blonde hair stood less than two feet from him. My gaze volleyed between the woman and Tucker.

I knew that face. She was a little older but just as stunning.

"Tucker, what's going on?"

Before he could answer, the woman stepped forward and held out her perfectly manicured hand. Red polish matched her red lips. "Hi, I'm Holly. And you are?"

Is this a fucking joke?

"Shit," Tucker muttered.

I ignored her hand and glared at Tucker.

"Well, this is a little awkward. I think I'll go grab a cup of coffee." Holly stepped into Tucker's space. She placed her hand on Tucker's bicep and gave it a squeeze. "I'll see you later." She stepped around me. Her heels clacked across the concrete floor as she made her exit.

I shut the door and spun on him. "What the fuck, Tucker? You said she was irrelevant."

"Cam—"

"Don't."

He ran his hands through his hair. "It's not a big deal. She came home for the holidays and brought her mom's car in to get the oil changed. I've been servicing her parents' cars for years."

"Given the way she touched you, it doesn't look like that's the only thing you've been servicing."

"That's bullshit, and you know it." He folded his arms over his chest and took a step forward. "It's business."

"Business that requires you to close your office door and have Nash watch Shayne?" My stance mirrored his. "Tucker, who the fuck is she?"

"My ex."

"Ex what?"

"Girlfriend." He dropped his arms and began to pace.

"Was it serious?"

"Very."

His quick honest answer would've stung, but I was too pissed.

"Let me get this straight. You're behind closed doors with your very serious ex, and I'm supposed to be okay with that?"

"You are blowing this way out of proportion. What? You think I was in here, fucking her? I'm not Jared," he roared.

I flinched.

He blew out a hard breath and lowered his voice. "She was talking about Dani, and I didn't want Shayne to overhear."

"Did you love her?" I had to know, but I was terrified of the answer.

"God, Camryn, do you hear yourself?" He had the balls to act insulted. "I love you, and any love I ever felt for Holly died a long fucking time ago."

"Really? Then, why do I get the feeling that Dani, even though she was your wife, isn't the one who really broke you?"

"Because she isn't." His confession cut like a knife.

A knock sounded on the door, and Nash walked in. "Are you two about done? Shayne is chomping at the bit."

"Yeah."

"No," Tucker said at the same time.

I folded my arms over my chest.

"This conversation isn't over," Tucker growled but not loud enough for anyone besides me and maybe Nash to hear.

I pointed through the doorway and spoke quietly, "That little girl has been looking forward to this all week. Do you want to go out there and tell her it's not happening?"

He was silent.

"I didn't think so." It was my turn to blow out a hard breath. I plastered a smile on my face and walked out of his office. My eyes went to Shayne. "Hey, sweet girl, go give Daddy hugs, so we can go."

"Yay!" she exclaimed around a mouthful of mints.

"Camryn"—Nash kept his voice low—"I know it looks bad, and there are things you don't know, but Tucker loves you."

"Can you handle the car seat, or do you want me to get it?" Tucker asked as he walked out of his office with Shayne on his heels.

I was glad for the interruption because I didn't want to have to figure out how to respond to Nash's comment.

"If the truck is unlocked, I'll handle it." I didn't bother meeting Tucker's gaze.

He tried to close the space between us, but I didn't give him the chance. It wasn't something that could be swept under the rug or fixed with a simple apology. I reached for Shayne's hand and walked out the door.

Less than ten minutes later, Shayne was buckled into her car seat in my car, and we were on our way to St. Charles, a neighboring town but much bigger than Jaxson Cove. Shayne chattered away in the backseat, and I only half-listened. Instead, I replayed the entire conversation with Tucker.

I pulled up to a stoplight and waited for it to turn green.

"Camryn? Hello? Camryn? Are you playing the quiet game?"

"I'm sorry, sweet girl. I was just thinking. Did you need something?" My eyes flitted to the rearview mirror as I made my turn.

"Can we—"

Tires squealed.
Glass shattered.
Screams filled my ears.
The world went black.

34

CAMRYN

Pain ricocheted through my head as the faint voices around me grew louder. Something soft pressed against my neck, but I couldn't tell what it was.

Fingers maybe?

I forced my eyes open a crack. Flashing red and blue lights assailed my vision, and I slammed my eyes shut, succumbing to the pounding ache in my skull.

Beep.

Something tightened around my arm, squeezing harder until my hand tingled. There was a clicking noise, followed by a whoosh of air that reminded me of the sound a tire made when the air pressure on the value stem released.

I tried to think, figure out where I was. The last thing I remembered was being in the car with Shayne.

Shayne.

Where is she?

I bolted upright. The room spun, and waves of nausea rolled over me. "Shayne? Shayne!"

"Camryn. Shh. It's okay."

A figure loomed in front of me. I blinked away the wetness blurring my vision.

"Nash?" My voice quaked. "Shayne. Where is she? Please tell me she's okay."

A woman dressed in scrubs and wearing glasses rushed into the room.

"Take it easy, Camryn. Everything's going to be okay." She checked the monitors and typed something into the electronic chart she held in her grasp. "I'm Robin, your nurse. Do you know where you are?"

"A hospital."

"Do you know why you're here?"

It all came flooding back. I had been making a protected left turn, and the other car had come out of nowhere.

"Car accident."

"That's right. You have a concussion and a few bumps and bruises, so we're just going to keep you for a little while for observation. Your vitals are good, though your heart rate is a little fast, which is to be expected."

"Please, the little girl who was in the car with me. Is she okay?" Tears fell down my face.

"Camryn," Nash spoke.

My eyes darted to him.

"I'll be right back to check on you," Robin said and then left the room.

Nash got up and paced at the foot of the bed. The small space prohibited him from making long strides.

"Nash, what are you not telling me?"

"The passenger side of the car sustained the brunt of the impact. Shayne hit her head pretty hard. There's a little swelling in her brain."

"No. No. No. I have to get out of here. I need to see her. Where are my clothes?" Each word became more frantic.

My fingers dug at the fabric cuff around my arm. I scratched against the Velcro, and when I found purchase, I ripped it off.

"Camryn, stop. Just stop."

Something in his voice made me settle back onto the bed.

"Tucker is taking care of Shayne. Laura and Macy are with him. You have a concussion. Just chill the hell out."

"What floor is she on?"

"Cam—"

"Nash," I bit out. Pain shot up the back of my skull, and I gripped my head in my hands. With my eyes squeezed shut, I sharply inhaled and then used all my strength to pin him with a menacing glare, which hurt like hell, but I wanted to get my point across. "I swear, if you don't tell me where she is, as soon as I'm released, I'll march my ass all over every inch of this entire fucking hospital until I find her."

I knew I wasn't her mother, but I loved her, and I couldn't lose her. Or Tucker. I'd just found them. It was going to be okay. All that mattered right now was Shayne.

"Here I thought, Macy was the most stubborn woman I'd ever met." He let out an exasperated sigh. "Fourth floor."

Six hours later, with my walking papers signed and Nash's promise that I wouldn't be driving home, I was free to go.

"Camryn"—there was a softness in the way he said my name as we left the emergency room area—"let me take you home, or I can take you to Macy's. Somebody should stay with you tonight."

Tone low and fierce, I told him, "I'm not leaving. I have to see Shayne. I need to make sure Tucker is okay." Instead of heading to the exit, I ambled toward the bank of elevators.

The fingers of Nash's free hand wrapped around my elbow, halting my steps. "He needs time."

That was when I knew. "He blames me." My watery gaze met Nash's eyes.

He didn't say a word. He didn't have to because his silence confirmed the truth.

"I love them, Nash. And, even if Tucker hates me, I can't walk out on them. If he do-does"—my voice cracked—"doesn't want me here." Tears streamed down my face. "He'll have to throw me out." I shrugged from his grip and continued to my destination.

Reflective silver doors distorted my image like mirrors at a carnival fun house as I stood in front of them, a squatty light-blue smear. Robin, the nurse, had found a pair of scrubs for me. My clothes had been covered in the tiniest shards of glass from the shattered windshield, so I couldn't wear them. I was glad I couldn't see what I really looked like. Between pain meds, adrenaline, and soul-consuming worry, I couldn't feel more than a headache.

With my index finger, I pressed the up arrow several times.

"You know, you only need to do that once." Nash's voice came from beside me. "People always push it repeatedly, and it doesn't make it get here any sooner."

"What are you doing?"

The doors slid open, and we stepped inside.

He held up a plastic bag that contained my belongings.

"Oh," I said and reached to take it from him.

He switched the bag to his other hand. "I've got it."

"Nash, what are you doing?" I repeated, thankful we were alone in the elevator.

"You need a friend," he remarked simply.

We exited onto the fourth floor, and I followed Nash down the corridor until he came to a stop in the doorway of a waiting room.

"Room four thirteen." He pointed the way. "I'll be waiting."

"Thanks."

My feet shuffled down the hall toward Shayne's room as though boulders had been strapped to my ankles. Out of every emotion that warred for ground, the one that won out was fear.

Is Shayne going to make it?

Will she be okay?

Does Tucker hate me?

The only thing greater than all my fears was the love and concern for the well-being of a little girl who had smiled and sassed her way into my heart.

When you looked at the big picture, Tucker and Shayne hadn't been in my life long. Months was a far cry from years. But love was a powerful and strange thing. There was no rhyme or reason. Love just was. It could take people months or sometimes even years to grasp what their soul had known in seconds.

The day my car wouldn't start and Shayne had told her dad I was a witch, it was a done deal. I loved that little girl with my whole heart. She had to be okay.

I mustered the last of my strength as I stopped in front of the door to Shayne's room and eased it open. Light filtered into the dark space, illuminating the small lump in the middle of the hospital bed.

35

TUCKER

There was no sense of time as I sat in the darkness. Eyes fluctuating between the glow of the monitor screens a foot away and the tiny being they were connected to. Age-old guilt sat in the center of my chest, nearly crushing me beneath the weight. To think there was a time I'd resented my daughter churned like acid in my gut.

The first time I'd held Bug in my arms, something had shifted inside me.

Loss after loss, I'd fought until I came out the other side because Shayne needed me.

But if I lose her ...

I pressed the pads of my thumbs against my eyelids, pushing back the wetness.

Rage burned just below the surface. *She* had done this. This was Camryn's fault.

Light filtered into the room, and then just as quickly, it was dark again. My eyes had long since adjusted, which gave me the advantage. Heavy, laden steps inched across the tiled floor. I knew it was her without even turning around.

She came to a stop at the foot of the bed. Her hand

covered her mouth, and when she shook her head back and forth, I caught the dampness that shone on her cheeks. She was crying.

Well, isn't that fucking rich?

I crossed my arms. "Leave."

Seemingly unaware of my presence, she jolted. "I'm sorry, Tucker." The apology was thick with emotion. "I'm so sorry."

The sight of her made me sick. "Sorry?" I laughed humorlessly. "You're sorry?"

She leaned forward, stretching out her hand to touch the form beneath the blanket.

I rose from my chair so fast, it skidded back a few inches. The loud noise bounced off the walls. I shoved Camryn's wrist before it made contact.

"Don't touch her." The words came out in a low growl, and she recoiled.

"Tucker."

"She's lying there because of you."

"It was an accident."

"Was it?" I ignored the tears that flowed endlessly from her eyes. I was too angry with her to care. "Were you focused on the road or too fucking jealous to see straight?"

The hold on my temper was slipping. For every step I took forward, she stepped back.

Until she didn't have anywhere left to go and she was backed against the bathroom door.

"Tucker, please. I'm so sorry."

I dropped my voice into a low, harsh whisper. "This," I pointed to the bed where Shayne lay but didn't take my eyes from hers as I spoke, "is your fault." Tears leaked from the corners of my own eyes as I struggled to get the words out. "Sh-she—fuck." I exhaled sharply and forced the words out.

"She is all I have left of them. And, if she isn't okay, I will never forgive you."

Her eyes bored into me. I ignored the devastation in their depths. Disregarded the questions I saw in those pools of blue.

Delicate hands fisted my shirt. Sobs racked her body.

The same body I'd once seen as a sanctuary was now the reason for my pain.

I removed her hands from my chest. "Get out."

I took a step away, but she didn't move.

I wanted to scream at her. Use my words to break her. To unleash every ounce of madness and hurt. If I did that, I would be running the risk of being thrown out of the hospital. I reeled in the last of my control. I didn't want to get thrown out of the hospital.

Quiet but forceful, I spoke, "So, help me God, if you don't leave, I will have you escorted out."

Just then, the door opened, and Nash walked inside.

I fixed my eyes on him but pointed to Camryn. "Get her the fuck out of my sight."

"It was an accident, Tuck. She doesn't deserve this."

"Really? Both of you, get out." I strode over to the chair, moved it closer to Shayne's bed, and took a seat.

Nash shook his head. "You're going to regret this, brother." He put an arm around Camryn and ushered her from the room.

As I sat in the darkness, my anger evaporated, and grief took its place. For the very first time in six years, I mourned all that I'd lost. I wept for my brother who never had the chance to be a father. For Dani, my best friend, who had lost the only man she ever loved while carrying their child. One she never had the chance to raise because, as strong as she had been, in the end, cancer had been stronger.

The words Nash had said when he walked out the door were true, but I couldn't think about Camryn right now or what I might regret later. Shayne was all I saw, and she had to be okay. Because I couldn't deal with the alternative.

I wiped the wetness from my face and leaned over to place a hand on my sleeping daughter. That was right.

My daughter.

She was mine. Legally and in every way that really mattered.

"You're okay, Bug. Daddy's here," I whispered into the stillness. Over and over again with my head against the mattress and her hand in my grasp.

Six years' worth of silent tears rolled across my nose and onto the blanket.

"You're okay. Daddy's here." With the words still on my lips, I fell asleep.

36

CAMRYN

The pounding in my head intensified. I held my head in between the heels of my palms and applied pressure to counteract the ache. On a deep inhale, I peeled open my eyes and immediately regretted it. Pain shot through my head as the stream of daylight burst against my pupils.

"Oh God." On a groan, I lifted my head and tried not to throw up. My eyes slowly traveled over the space.

I was in my living room on the couch, and Nash was passed out in the chair.

Nash?

Something was off. I glanced down and saw the blue scrubs I was wearing. Every part of my body ached like I'd been hit by a truck.

Memories of the last several hours flooded back. The accident. Shayne.

"Nash. Nash!" The shrill of my own voice brought on a new wave of agony.

He jumped up. "What? What is it?"

"Shayne."

"Camryn, calm down. It's still early. The doctors probably haven't even made their rounds yet."

Overwhelmed by sadness and fear, I began to cry.

"Shit. Don't cry. I'll check my phone."

I watched as he fished it from his back pocket, unlocked the screen, and scrolled.

When he looked up, the answer was written all over his face. "She hasn't woken up yet."

Nausea washed over me. As painful as it was, I scrambled from the couch to the bathroom and emptied the contents of my stomach.

Several minutes later, Macy appeared in the doorway.

"Hey, Rocky."

My head lay on the crook of my arm that was draped over the toilet seat. "When did you get here?"

"A few minutes ago. You look like shit. Let's get you to bed. Can you help me, or do I need to get Nash?"

"I can do it." My head spun like a merry-go-round when I tried to get up, and I crumbled to the floor.

"Nash," Macy hollered, and I groaned. "Sorry," she apologized. When Nash appeared at the door, Macy asked, "Will you help me get her to her room?"

"Sure." Nash bent down and carefully scooped me into his arms. He carried me into my room and gently set me on my bed.

Then, they talked about me like I wasn't in the room.

"Maybe she needs to go back to the hospital? You said she has a concussion. Throwing up can't be good."

"I'm not sure when she ate last, and Tucker was an asshole last night. Maybe it's related."

Slowly, I curled into the fetal position. "He hates me." My voice was so small.

"Camryn ..." Macy trailed off.

"It's true," I said matter-of-factly. "I don't blame him. It's my fault. I just want Shayne to be okay."

"She'll be fine." There wasn't a trace of doubt in Nash's voice, and I clung to it like a beacon of hope.

Tucker's words from last night came back to me.

"She is all I have left of them."

Them.

Those four little letters wreaked havoc on my brain. I tried to make sense of them and couldn't. Sleep pulled me under again. Unable to keep my eyes open any longer, I gave up the fight.

The next time I came to, I heard the low rumble of voices from the other room. My headache was better, but the rest of my body ached. With careful movements, I got out of bed and made my way to my bedroom door. I twisted the knob and ambled toward the sound of voices.

Nash and Grayson sat at my kitchen island, and Macy was nowhere in sight.

Grayson?

Maybe I should ask Nash to drive me back to the hospital.

I shuffled into the kitchen. "Grayson?" I asked in disbelief.

"There's my girl." He came over and gave me the gentlest hug. Then, he stood protectively at my side.

"Okay, so you two do know each other," Nash said and slid from his stool. He crossed the space separating us.

A look passed between the two men, and Nash held up his hands. "Look, man, there was no fucking way I was leaving you alone with her without verification."

Grayson offered his hand to Nash. "I respect the hell out of you for that, man."

They shook hands, and then Nash turned his focus to me. He put a hand on each of my upper arms, as if to hold me upright. "Tucker called. Shayne's okay."

"What? She is?" I smiled through my tears. "Oh my God. Is she okay? I mean, really okay?"

"She's already asking for ice cream." He chuckled. "She's fine."

"Oh my God." I fell into Nash's chest and wept from sheer relief.

After a few minutes, Nash passed me off to Grayson. "Since you're in good hands, I'm going to head out."

"Are you going to the hospital? Let me grab my—"

"I can't," Nash cut off my words. "Fuck. I'm sorry, Camryn. He doesn't want to see you."

"Right. Will you tell her ..." It took extreme effort to push past the thick emotion that clogged my throat. "T-tell her t-that I love her, and can you t-tell t-them b-both t-that I'm s-so-sorry?"

"I will. I promise." His gaze slid to Grayson and then back to me. "Give him some time, Camryn. He loves you, and he'll come around. Don't give up on him."

Nash sauntered to the front door, and I called out to him, "Hey."

He twisted to face me with his brow raised.

"Tucker said something last night, and it doesn't make sense."

"What's that?"

"He said, Shayne was all he had left of *them*," I emphasized the word. "What does that mean? Who is *them*?"

Nash's eyes grew wide as saucers. He muttered something under his breath that I couldn't quite make out. "It's not my story to tell. Macy will check on you later."

And, with that, he walked out the door.

The picture. The six of them. Griffin and Dani. Tucker and Holly. Nash and Macy.

Them.

Like puzzle pieces locking into place, it all became so clear.

37

TUCKER

Shayne had been unconscious at the scene, and the CT scan had shown she had a mild brain contusion as well as other bruises and a few scrapes. They'd given her pain meds, and all she'd done was sleep.

The worry drove me to the edge of sanity.

I ran my hands through my hair and paced the same ten squares of gleaming white tiles. When I grew tired of doing that, I stood in front of the window. The streets below were bustling with cars as the world carried on beyond the thick glass. Everyone else was going on with their lives while I had been dropped into my worst nightmare.

"Daddy?"

I whirled around to see hazel eyes, the same shade as mine and Griffin's, staring up at me. It'd been hours since I saw those eyes. I couldn't get to her side fast enough.

"Doodlebug. You're awake." I mashed the call button for the nurse.

"Hi, Daddy."

Relief welled up inside me and ran down my cheeks. "Hi, Bug."

Her lip trembled.

Shit.

I needed to pull it together. I was probably scaring her to death. "It's okay, baby."

"Are we in the hospital?"

"Yes. But you're okay," I rushed to add.

The nurse—I thought her name was Elizabeth—strolled over to the bed. "Hey, Miss Shayne. Did you have a nice nap?"

"I guess so."

"See this finger?" Elizabeth asked, and Shayne nodded. "Okay. I want you to look at my finger and follow it with your eyes."

She did as the nurse had asked.

"Good job. I bet I have some stickers at the nurses' station. Would you like me to bring you one?"

Shayne smiled sweetly. "Do you have ice cream at the nurses' station?"

Elizabeth and I both laughed.

"I'll see what I can do," she said, typing something into Shayne's electronic chart before she left the room.

"Daddy, is Camryn okay?"

Fuck.

The question twisted like a knife in my gut.

What am I supposed to tell her? Why isn't this shit covered in all those damn baby books?

Her eyes filled with tears. "I want Camryn. Where is she?" Shayne's bottom lip jutted out, and fat tears rolled down her sweet face.

Camryn isn't here because I threw her out. I said horrible things to her, and I blamed her for something that wasn't her fault.

I wiped her tears with my thumb. "Don't cry, Bug. How

about I call Uncle Nash and see if he can bring Wilbur up here? Would you like that?"

"Okay." She sniffed.

A few minutes later, Elizabeth returned with Shayne's ice cream the same time my mom came in with two coffees. I'd never been so glad to have reinforcement. With a promise to Shayne that I'd be right back, I stepped from the room to call Nash.

38

CAMRYN

Six days had passed since the accident. Tucker had made it perfectly clear the night in the hospital that we were done. I knew he didn't want to see me, so Nash and Macy kept me in the loop about Shayne. My body was recovering, but I doubted my heart ever would. I missed Tucker like crazy, even after everything he'd said. It didn't matter how much he blamed me because it would never equate to how much I blamed myself.

I played the accident on a constant loop in my head. I was plagued with vivid nightmares where all those different what-if scenarios came to life.

Shayne trapped in a burning car. Tucker's and Holly's faces screaming at me that it was my fault.

Shayne covered in shattered glass, begging me to help her.

The images lingered in my mind long after I woke up.

Shayne was supposed to come home today. More than anything, I yearned to see her with my own eyes. To wrap her in my arms and hold on to her for dear life. I needed proof that she was okay and that she didn't hate me. As badly as I wanted it, I knew Tucker probably wouldn't let it happen, and I didn't get a say in the matter.

I didn't know what I would've done without Grayson to keep my mind off things. He'd entertained me with tales from his travels and made me laugh even in the shittiest of circumstances. A few days ago, he had taken me car shopping. It had taken an entire day, but I'd found something newer that I could afford, and it was a lot more reliable than Lucille had been. She was just a car. A hunk of metal that could be replaced, but it was also one less piece I had of my dad.

Before Grayson had left yesterday, he'd invited me to go with him to South Carolina for the holidays to visit his family. As much as I'd appreciated the invite, I'd make miserable company. Instead, I decided to get out of town for a few days. I didn't know where I was going, but I knew I couldn't be here. Not when Tucker didn't want me. Not after everything he said to me.

I wheeled my suitcase into the living room, put my purse over my shoulder, and grabbed my keys. I locked the door behind me and kept my eyes trained on the ground until I heard that sweet voice.

"Camryn!" she yelled with her arms wide open while she ran toward me.

Oh my God. She was here, and she wanted me. I dropped my purse and keys onto the driveway and caught her. The second her arms wrapped around my neck, she burst into tears, and I carefully lowered us to the ground.

She hugged me so tight; her small arms were like a vise.

I rocked her in my arms and stroked her hair. "Shh. Don't cry, sweet girl. It's okay." It felt so good to hold her. The roller coaster of emotions peaked, and salty rivers poured from my face.

"You did-didn't c-come to see me at the h-hospital," she wailed.

Tucker's form blurred before me while a sob ripped from my throat. I wanted to scream at him. To rage against him and tell him how fucking wrong this was. And that I would never forgive him.

How could he do this?

To her?

To us?

"I'm sorry, kiddo. I'm so sorry."

I tried to adjust her body, so I could look at her, but she wouldn't let go.

"Daddy said you were okay. But you n-never c-came."

"Shayne, it's okay. I'm sorry, baby girl."

I wanted to throw Tucker under the bus. Tell this broken little girl that her daddy wouldn't let me come to the hospital because he didn't want to see me.

She lifted her head to look at me. "I t-thought y-you did-didn't w-wa-want—" She was sobbing so hard, she could hardly breathe. "I thought you did-didn't want me any-anymore."

I laid her head on my shoulder and rested my cheek on top. Then, I cried harder than I'd ever cried in my life.

I no longer wanted to scream at Tucker. I wanted to kick his ass.

He knelt beside us. "Bug, come on," he said gently.

She moved her head to my other shoulder, away from her father, and tightened her grip.

I glared at him through the most epic ugly cry in history. Then, I pointed to Shayne and mouthed, *This is your fault.*

He didn't respond. He didn't have to because, from the look on his face, it was the truth.

Slowly, I rose to my feet, careful not to drop Shayne.

"No. Hold me. Please, Camryn."

This kid was breaking all the parts of me that had already been broken. "I've got you. Shh. It's okay."

She needed to be held, and she was exhausted. I couldn't handle Tucker being in my space, and besides, he was the one with a rocking chair.

I jerked my head in the direction of his house. "Go open your door."

Tucker wasn't the kind of man who took orders from anyone, but I had zero fucks to give.

He collected my things and led the way to his house.

39

TUCKER

I opened the door and stepped out of the way to allow Camryn to pass. Shayne was still clinging to her like a second skin, but at least she'd calmed down a little.

Camryn made herself comfortable in my recliner and began to rock Bug. "Hey, sweet girl," she murmured. "Do you want to know a secret?"

Shayne nodded against Camryn's chest.

"Can you look at me?" Camryn waited for Shayne's red-rimmed eyes to meet hers. "I love you. Do you know that?"

"Y-yes."

"You are my very best friend, and I will never, ever not want you. Okay?"

"Okay." Shayne let out a yawn. "I'm so sleepy."

The kid had been through a lot recently, and after that, I was sure it was normal.

"Want me to rock you?"

"Yes. Will you be here when I wake up?"

I watched their exchange, feeling like a voyeur in my own house, but I had to know.

Shame and guilt had been my constant companions. I

wanted to fix what I had broken. The sight of them as they'd sat in the driveway, clinging to each other, slayed me. Watching them now tore at the shreds of my heart. Camryn had every right to never speak to me again. Instead of pulling her close, I'd pushed her away like she hadn't meant anything to me.

As if she could read my mind, Camryn looked at me, and the pain I saw in her blue eyes was tangible. She didn't answer Shayne's question. Instead, she said, "How about you close your eyes for a little bit? Do you want your dad to grab you a blanket?"

She made a fist and then rubbed her eye. "Will you, Daddy? And Wilbur, too."

I went into Shayne's bedroom and grabbed everything she'd asked for. I took it back to the living room. While Camryn rocked my daughter, she hummed softly, and within less than ten minutes, Bug was snoring quietly in her arms. After a few more minutes, when Camryn was certain Shayne was sound asleep, she managed to get up from the chair and carry her into her bedroom. She settled the blanket over her and dropped a kiss to her forehead before exiting the room.

I was on her heels as she made it to my front door.

"Can we talk?"

"No. Whatever it is, I don't want to hear it," she cried. "How could you, Tucker? If you wanted to hurt me, congratulations. You've succeeded. By keeping me away"—she angrily swatted at her tears—"you let her believe that I abandoned her. That I didn't want her. I'm so fucking angry with you for that. I wanted to be there, but you didn't want me. There isn't a thing you can say to justify what you did."

"So, that's it?"

Camryn twisted the knob, opened the door, and stepped onto the porch. "You said you were done, remember?"

"Damn it, Camryn. I was scared to death, and I wasn't thinking straight. I'm sorry."

She spun on her heels and glowered at me. "So am I, Tucker. I'm sorry I let myself believe you were different. I'm sorry that I let you in. Most of all, I'm so fucking sorry I ever fell in love with you."

"You don't mean that."

"You're right," she sobbed. "I don't, and I'm sorry about that most of all. Because there isn't anything I wouldn't give right now to hate you." She grabbed her stuff, gave me her back, and walked away.

40

CAMRYN

By the time I crossed the lawn between our houses, my vision was so blurry, I could barely make out the ground in front of me. I unlocked my front door and went inside. After I closed the door behind me, and dropped my stuff in the living room, I toed off my shoes and headed to my bedroom. I sank down onto my mattress, curled into a ball, and cried myself to sleep.

Hours later, after a hot bath and a bottle of wine, I sent Tucker a text.

Me: How is she?
Tucker: She ate half of a grilled cheese, and she's watching Beauty and the Beast. Want to come over?
Me: No.

Emotionally spent and too tipsy and tired to go anywhere, I decided to wait until tomorrow to leave.

I awoke to someone knocking on the front door. Unless it was someone holding a million-dollar sweepstakes cardboard check, I was about to be arrested for murder.

With a scowl affixed to my face, I unlocked the door and swung it open. "Hel—"

Nobody was there. A split second before a string of curses left my lips, I heard giggling.

"Down here, silly." Shayne snickered. "Do you want to go out to breakfast with us?"

Tucker appeared behind her, arms folded and sexy grin plastered on his perfect face. My eyes trailed across his thick veins of his forearms, and my tongue darted out to lick my lips.

Asshole. He knows exactly what he is doing.

I glared at him with a look that said, *You don't play fair.*

Mirth danced in his eyes, and he shrugged.

"Please," Shayne said and thrust out her bottom lip.

I put my index finger to her lip and flicked downward. "You know, one of these days, that isn't going to work, right?"

"It is not this day," she retorted.

Tucker roared with laughter.

I ruffled Shayne's hair. "Oh my God, you really are too much." I laughed. "Give me five minutes to get dressed."

I stepped out of the way and allowed them inside. I went to change.

Before I was out of earshot, I heard Shayne say, "See, Daddy? It really is a superpower."

Laura met us at Pancake Palace for breakfast. The situation could've been awkward, but it wasn't—at least, not until I realized I'd been played. After we ate, Laura took Shayne back to her house under the guise of decorating the Christmas tree, leaving Tucker and me alone together.

I was such an idiot. I should've driven myself.

"I just want to talk," Tucker said from his spot across the booth.

I stared out the large picture window. "So, talk."

"Not here. Let's go for a drive."

"I need to be home in an hour."

"Okay."

Tension filled the cab of his truck as we drove out to the beach. There was a nip in the air from the ocean breeze. When we got out of the truck, Tucker wrapped a small throw blanket over my shoulders, and I fought the urge to lean into his touch.

The beach was mostly deserted, except for a few stragglers. We walked for a few minutes, and then Tucker broke the silence.

"When I was younger, I couldn't get out of Jaxson Cove fast enough. Holly was a free spirit, and we were high school sweethearts. After we graduated, with a little money in our pockets, we left."

"Who ran the garage?"

"Between my mom and a few longtime employees, the garage practically ran itself." He shoved his hands in his pockets. "When I got the call about Griff ..." He cleared his throat.

I knew this wasn't easy for him, and the need to comfort him in some small way was too strong to deny. So, I linked my arm through his and curved my fingers over his bicep.

"When I got the call," he repeated, "we took the first flight home. Mom was a mess, and Dani was three and a half months pregnant. After a few weeks, Holly wanted her life back, but I couldn't leave. Everything and everyone around me was falling apart, and I had to fix it."

"Tucker, I'm so sorry."

"Every chance Holly had, she told me how much she hated it here. When I refused to go with her, she left."

"What a bitch!" I regretted it instantly. "I shouldn't have said that. I'm sorry."

"Don't be. It's the fucking truth."

"We found out about Dani's cancer as her pregnancy progressed. She refused treatment because she didn't want to lose the baby. Next to Griffin, Dani was my best friend in the entire world. I promised her I'd take care of her and the baby."

Tears stung my eyes. This man was shattering my resolve with every word that fell from his lips.

"Do you want to sit?" Tucker pointed his finger toward the pier about twenty feet away.

"Sure."

He was quiet until we were situated on the edge of the dock. When he slipped an arm around me and brought me into his side, I let him. I knew deep in my gut that he needed this to be able to get through the rest of his story.

"One night, it all got to be too much, and I called Holly … asked her to come home." He moved his arm from around me, leaned forward with his elbows on his knees, and stared into the water. "I was terrified. The longer Dani put off treatment, the more likely it was that she wouldn't make it. I didn't know shit about raising a kid. And my mom was a basket case. Do you want to know what Holly said?"

It was a rhetorical question, so I didn't answer.

"She said she had just started a new job at a dance club in Vegas, and it wasn't a good time."

White-hot rage clouded the edge of my vision, and if that selfish, prissy little bitch were standing in front of me,

I'd shove her ass off the edge of the pier into the ocean below.

"Was she always like that? God, she sounds like a wretched person."

"She is. That's another reason my office door was closed that day. I couldn't subject Bug to that."

"Tucker …"

"I know. I just needed to say it." He absently picked at a loose thread on his jeans. "Anyway, Dani didn't have family, and she needed a support system. When she was eight months pregnant, we got married. My name is on Shayne's birth certificate." A sad smile tugged at the corner of his mouth. "Griffin's middle name was Shane. Dani just spelled it differently."

I didn't even know what to say.

He turned his torso toward me and took my hands in his. "I resented my brother for a long time—and not just him, but Shayne, too." Shame blanketed his features. "Between the endless nights of taking care of Dani, trying to keep my mom from swallowing a bottle of pills, and running the garage, I was barely hanging on. There was nobody for me to lean on, and I resented having to raise a kid I'd never asked for on top of it all." His eyes shone, and I pulled my hands from his grasp to wrap him in a hug.

"I'm sorry, baby. I'm so fucking sorry I hurt you." He pressed his lips against my head.

"Tucker …"

He leaned away and met my gaze. "Camryn, what I said to you is unforgivable. I was so consumed with my own demons, and I took all of it out on you."

"I need a little time to process all of this."

He stood and then held out his hand to pull me to my

feet, and he didn't let it go. We walked hand in hand over the wooden slats.

Once we were on the sand, he cupped my cheeks and caught my gaze. "I know you need time, but I'm not going down without a fight. I love you, and I'm going to lose you."

41

CAMRYN

It had been over a month since Tucker poured his heart out on the beach. We spent endless hours just talking nearly every night after Shayne went to sleep. Each day, he would give me little pieces of himself, and I would try to do the same in return. When I tumbled too close to the edge and tried to pull away, there he was, fighting for me. I had accepted his apology that day on the dock, but I hadn't been able to truly forgive him—until now.

Laura was keeping Shayne for the weekend, and Tucker would be here in twenty minutes. The wine was uncorked, dinner was in the oven, and I just needed to make a salad to go with it.

While I waited for Tucker, I poured myself a glass of wine, pulled up my playlist, and got to work on gathering ingredients for a Greek salad. It didn't take long to throw it together. As I bent to put it in the fridge, I felt Tucker's presence behind me.

I turned and found him leaning against the wall with hunger in his eyes and a smirk on his lips.

He crossed the space between us and drew me into his embrace. "I missed you, baby."

I snuggled into him and let his words wash over me.

With a finger hooked under my chin, he tilted my head and ghosted a kiss across my lips. I melted into him, seeking more of his touch. A hand went to the back of my neck, and he dived his tongue inside my mouth. My body blazed with need, his kiss consuming me from the inside out. I slid my hands beneath his shirt and moaned when the heat of his chest met my palms.

Tucker lifted me into his arms without breaking the seal of our lips. He kissed me until I was near breathless.

"Baby?"

We hadn't had sex in a while. Since before the accident. He was asking permission, and there was no way I could deny him. Deny myself any longer.

"Yes."

With that single word, he carried me into the bedroom and laid me down on the bed. He tugged off his shirt and toed off his shoes but left his jeans on.

The intense way he looked at my body made me want to hide beneath the covers.

"I never want you to hide from me, Camryn," he said, reading my thoughts. "You're stunning, and I like my shirt on you." He smirked. He knelt on the end of the bed, grabbed the backs of my thighs, and tugged me closer. "Of course, I think you'd look even better out of it."

He started at the bottom, undoing the buttons one by one. The shirt lay open, my bare breasts exposed. Tucker dipped his head and lavished each of my pebbled nipples with attention. Every swirl of his tongue heated my skin.

I moaned his name.

"I need to hear you say it."

All my defenses were down. "Make love to me."

With that, he stripped out of his jeans faster than a man of his size should be able to. I freed myself from the confines of his shirt and glided my panties down my legs.

He slipped a finger inside me. "So wet, baby."

After he licked my taste from his finger, he crawled up my body and reached into the nightstand for a foil packet. He sheathed his cock, positioned himself at my entrance and eased inside inch by glorious inch.

From the way he moved his body, I knew he wanted to make it last. He stared down at me with a love so deep and intense that I couldn't look away. We used our bodies to speak the words we didn't know how to form.

I bucked into him, and he began to move faster. My legs locked around his lower back. The change in position sent him deeper.

I wiggled a hand between us and began to rub circles. "Yes. Oh God, Tucker."

I barreled toward my climax, and I cried out his name as I soared over the edge.

Tucker growled out his own release, and then he pulled me into his arms before collapsing next to me. He shifted my hair off my face. "I love you, baby."

"I love you, too, and I trust you with my heart."

He was quiet for several beats before he spoke again, "Camryn?" His warm breath danced over my skin.

"Yes?" I whispered.

"I'm keeping you."

The conviction in his words soothed all the cracks in my soul.

EPILOGUE

"Is it time for cake yet?"

"Presents first, Bug," Daddy said.

"Can I give Camryn my present first?"

"How about we save it for last?" Grammy suggested.

"Okay." I sat down at the table beside Camryn and stared at the birthday cake.

"Here you go, baby." My dad gave a tall, cylinder shaped gift to her.

I watched her tear off the paper and open the top. She turned it upside down, and papers slid out. Giant, rolled-up sheets of paper with a bunch of blue lines and squares on them. The page on top looked like a drawing of a house. Then, Camryn started to cry. I would've cried, too. Because let's face it; nobody wanted a tube full of papers for their birthday.

Camryn wiped her eyes and reached into her purse. "Here, this is for you."

She gave the present to Daddy, which didn't make any sense because he'd already had a birthday. He opened it up, and inside was a rectangular plastic stick with a little window and two pink lines on it.

Now, Daddy looked like he was going to cry. "Yeah?"

"Yep."

Daddy picked her up and twirled her around. "Oh shit," he said and set her back down.

I held my hand out for a quarter. If these two kept it up, I'd have a car by the time I was ten. I really wanted cake, so I decided to hurry things along. "Here you go." I gave Camryn a pretty package that I'd wrapped myself. I waited not-so patiently while she opened the fuzzy box.

She held up the necklace and started to cry.

Good grief.

"Look"—I pointed to the words—"it says *Mama* and has the number two for Mama squared. I already had a mommy, but in two more sleeps, you're going to be my second mommy. Why are you crying? Don't you like it?"

"I love it, sweet girl. These are happy tears."

"Happy tears? That must be something only grown-ups do. Can we have cake now?"

EPILOGUE

My heart was full as I took in my family from the spot where I stood on the back porch. I lived for moments like this. Cold beer in my hand, the sound of my children's laughter in my ears, and the sight of my beautiful wife in her element.

I watched Camryn gently push our son, Levi, in the plastic toddler swing while Bug swung beside them. She pumped her legs higher and higher, and I swore, she was going to catapult herself over the top bar of the damn swing set.

At seven years old, Shayne looked more like her mother every day. I saw a lot of Griffin in her, too. Griff and I'd looked a lot alike, but she had some of his mannerisms.

Most people in Jaxson Cove assumed Dani and I had sought solace in each other's arms when Griffin died, and Shayne had been a result of that. The truth was, from the moment Griffin and Dani had laid eyes on each other when we were kids, they'd belonged to one another. Dani might have been my wife, but it was only ever on paper. Her last request was that, when the time was right, I'd tell Shayne the truth. That was a secret only those closest to me knew and one I intended to take to my grave because no good would come from it.

"Mama?"

Shayne's voice pulled me from my thoughts.

Camryn smiled at our daughter. "Yes, sweet girl?"

"How much money do you think storm chasers make?"

Camryn looked thoughtful. "I'm not really sure, but we can Google it."

"I mean, I'm holding out for Jim Cantore's job, but I might need a plan B."

Unable to contain my laughter, a loud chuckle escaped, and I gave myself away.

"Dad's home," Shayne screeched, jumped off the swing, and raced in my direction.

I set my now-empty beer bottle down, met her at the bottom of the steps, and opened my arms. "Hey, Doodlebug. How was your day?"

She wrapped her arms around my neck and gave me a squeeze. "Amazing. We made tornadoes in a bottle in science class today." She kissed my cheek and then said, "I'm thirsty. I'll be right back."

She went inside, and I walked toward Camryn.

"I swear, one of these days, she's going to break a bone," she said as I approached. "Maybe two, given the way she jumps off that swing."

I wrapped my arms around her waist from behind and hugged her to me. I moved her hair to the side and nuzzled the sensitive spot just below her earlobe. "I missed you, baby."

She leaned her head back onto my shoulder. "I missed you, too." After a few beats, she looked down at Levi, who had fallen asleep in the swing. "I guess we'd better go inside, so I can start dinner."

I turned her around in my arms and tilted her face, so I could kiss her. It'd been hours since my mouth was on hers. I needed to taste her sweetness. I swept my lips over hers before nipping her bottom lip and gently tugging it between my teeth. My hand went to her nape as I dived inside her mouth. I slid my tongue against hers, stoking the flame that always burned white-hot between us. It took all the restraint I possessed not to strip her bare and carry her to the hammock, which sat mere feet away. The grip on my control slipped further away, and I broke the kiss before I did just that.

"Tucker."

I loved the sound of my name on her lips.

My gaze locked with hers. "Tonight, we'll put the kids down early, and then I'm going to spend hours with my face between your legs." My thumb skated over her cheek, and I leaned in closer. "And, after I've made you scream my name"—I dragged the pad of that same thumb over her bottom lip—"multiple times, I'm going to bury myself inside you and make love to you until the sun comes up."

"Promise?" She wove her fingers into my hair and tugged my mouth to hers.

"Promise," I vowed against her lips.

"Okay." She stepped out of my arms and started to reach for Levi before I stopped her.

"I've got him, baby. Go pour yourself a glass of wine and take a hot bath. I'll handle dinner."

"Really? Are you sure?"

"Yes." I swatted her backside. "Now, get."

She laughed, stood on her tiptoes, and planted a chaste kiss on my mouth. Then, she turned toward the house.

"Tucker"—she faced me but walked backward—"make sure to tell them to hold the black olives." Her tinkling giggle hit my ears. She knew me too well.

After Camryn went inside, I pulled out my phone and placed the pizza delivery order. Then, I turned my attention to my son. His black hair lifted slightly in the breeze as I continued to keep the swing in motion with the press of my fingers.

Peace and contentment washed over me as I took it all in. I had the house, the family, and, hell, I even had the white picket fence because I couldn't say no to my wife.

Levi started to fuss, and I lifted him out of the confines of the swing. "Shh, buddy. Daddy's here. I've got you," I soothed as I held him against my chest and rubbed circles on his back, the same way I had done with his big sister all those years ago.

Everything I thought I'd never wanted ended up being the very thing I could never live without.

ACKNOWLEDGMENTS

To God—The first portion.

To my readers—Without you, none of this would even be possible. Thank you for reading my words, sending me messages, and writing reviews. I appreciate each and every one of you.

To all the bloggers—Thank you so much for all the posts you've shared and how tirelessly you work on behalf of authors. I see you, I appreciate you, and I'm thankful for you.

Mr. Street, I love that you embrace my crazy. I love that you still look at me the way Prince Harry looks at Meghan, even when my shirt is covered in cheddar dust and I haven't showered in three days. Thank you for the way you love me. You are my happily ever after. I will love you until I breathe my last breath, and even then, I'll love you still. My cup runneth over. P.S. Still Arby's. You really should just admit I'm right.

Sunshine Girl, the third time is not a charm, and you can't read this book either, except for this part. There is so much of your personality in Shayne's character. You always wanted one more chapter, and I thought I was so cool, teaching you those big words—until you told me I was exasperating you ... and you were only two. I was a little too proud to be offended. There is nothing in this world I love more than being your mom. I'm so proud of you. I love you, Baby Bear, to the moon and back again, plus all the stars in the sky.

Mom, thank you for being one of my biggest cheerleaders. I love that you're so proud of me, but I'm not sure random strangers appreciate your enthusiasm. I'm certain the lady in the checkout line just wanted to pay for her milk and leave.

Tracy, sister dear, not much has changed since we were kids. Back then, I forced you to listen to my stories, and now, I make you read them. As far as sisters go, I could've done worse, and you couldn't have done better.

Family, thank you for not disowning me or being butthurt that I didn't name all of you individually. Also, I'll be that vaguely familiar-looking face at Sunday supper. I love every single one of you.

My girls, Marni and Crystal, thank you for being the most kick-ass girlfriends a woman could ever wish for. Through laughter and tears. Through trials and triumphs. Your friendship has never wavered. I love you both fiercely, and I'd be lost without you.

Marisol and Brittany, sometimes, your friend writes a book and has the audacity to steal your names.

Shayne Ryder, speaking of name-stealing, thanks for letting me use yours. And for not taking out a restraining order when I stalked you on social media. I hope you love Shayne's character as much as I do.

Jovana Shirley, you're a wonderful human and a remarkable editor. You turned all my ramblings and misplaced adjectives into something I'm incredibly proud of. I couldn't imagine doing this without you. Thank you ... for everything.

Shannon of Shanoff Designs, thank you for the amazing cover and for working so hard to catch my vision.

Tandy Proofreads, this was our first time working together, and I'm sure it won't be the last. Thank you for rising to the challenge and meeting a tight deadline. I appreciate you so much.

My betas—Marni, Crystal, Tracy, Dani, and Robin— thank you, and I appreciate your time more than you know. I'm a hot mess, and you put up with me despite it all.

Stacey, Tina, and Robin, thank you for answering all my questions. I appreciate you all so much.

Cary, RC, Hazel, Maria, Angelia, and Karin, I have mad love for you ladies.

K's Kartel, thank you for being the best reader group ever. Y'all are so supportive and know how to make a girl feel loved. Thank you for being on this journey with me.

To everyone who thinks they've been forgotten—Please know that, just because your names aren't printed here, it doesn't mean they're not written on my heart.

ABOUT THE AUTHOR

K. Street has been making up stories since she was old enough to talk and began writing at the tender age of eleven. She resides in central Florida with her husband and daughter. Her affinity for coffee, wine, dark chocolate, and hockey runs deep. When K isn't working or writing she enjoys reading, cooking, spending time with her family and cheering on her beloved Chicago Blackhawks.

Join her reader group, K's Kartel, by clicking: HERE

OTHER BOOKS BY K. STREET

Healing the Broken

The Fall of Cinderella

PREVIEW

Keep reading for a preview of The Fall of Cinderella

The Fall of Cinderella

K. STREET

PROLOGUE

TESSA

My heels clack against the tiles as I cross the lobby to meet my next client. He's tall with blond hair that falls just over his right eye. Even though he's wearing a suit and tie, he looks like he belongs on a surfboard in SoCal instead of standing inside the Art Institute of Chicago.

I smile warmly and extend my hand. "Good morning, Mr. Salinger. I'm Tessa Carmichael, the assistant event coordinator." My pulse races as his palm slides into mine.

"Good morning, Tessa. Please, call me Trevor." His voice is smooth and husky.

"If you'll join me in my office, I'll show you what I've got in mind for the gala." I gesture across the lobby.

As we walk, he asks, "So, how long have you been the assistant event coordinator?"

"Almost a year," I reply and open the office door. "You can have a seat if you'd like." I motion to the dark leather couch that faces the table where my laptop lies open. "Can I get you a bottle of water? Or a cup of coffee?"

He sits down, and his eyes slowly scan over the length of me before returning to my face. "Water would be great."

I open the mini fridge, withdraw two bottles of water, and give one to him. I watch him unscrew the cap and lift the bottle to his mouth. His tongue darts out to catch a droplet of water, and an audible gasp escapes me.

"Tessa? Everything okay?"

"Um, yes. I'm sorry." I desperately need to get control of my libido. I make sure to leave room between us when I take a seat on the couch and ask, "Do you have an updated head count?" I click open the Excel spreadsheet and wait for him to answer. When he doesn't, I look up to see his eyes fixed on my lips.

"Seven hundred," he answers seamlessly.

I enter the number and return my attention to him. "Did you bring a check for the deposit?"

He reaches into his gray suit jacket and withdraws a white envelope. When he extends it to me, our fingers brush. My breath catches, and I feel his touch all the way to my toes. Our gazes lock, and a current crackles through the air. I try to take the envelope from his hand, but he holds tightly to it.

"Tessa, have dinner with me." He doesn't phrase it like a question, and I'm certain it isn't a request.

"Mr. Salinger," I say. He raises an eyebrow at me. "Trevor, I'm sorry. I can't."

"You can't? As in you're not capable? Or you won't?"

"Won't. It's frowned upon. Sort of a conflict of interest."

"Meet me for a drink then."

"I—"

"One drink, Tessa. That's all," he says, cutting me off.

And damn if I don't love the way he says my name.

"Fine," I concede.

One drink leads to two. One dinner rolls into another,

and by the time the charity gala comes and goes, I'm falling in love with Trevor Salinger. The man is full of charm, and loving him comes as easy as breathing. Just like a fairy tale...

CHAPTER ONE

TESSA - FOUR AND A HALF YEARS LATER

Bam! Bam! Bam!

The pounding on the door jerks me from sleep, and it takes me a minute to get my bearings. I must have dozed off on the couch, waiting for Trevor to get home. Wiping sleep from my eyes, I stumble to the door as the banging sounds again.

"Mrs. Salinger?" a deep voice calls from the other side of the door.

"Just a minute. I'll be right there," I reply, striving to keep panic from my voice. It's late and dark and I don't recognize the voice.

With unsteady fingers, I comb through my hair and then run my flattened palms over my pajamas, smoothing them out. On my tiptoes, I peer through the peephole and see Theo, our doorman, standing in the hall. He's flanked by two officers from the Chicago Police Department. A sinking feeling settles into the pit of my gut as I twist the knob and open the door.

"Theo." My voice trembles as I say his name.

"It's all right, miss. These officers need a moment of your

time." He forces a smile, one I'm certain is meant for reassurance, but it doesn't help. Theo turns and then walks to the elevator without glancing back.

"Mrs. Salinger, may we come in?" one of the officers asks.

"I'm so sorry. Yes, of course, please come inside." I gesture to the living room and wait for them to step inside before closing the door. My feet are heavy as I follow behind them.

The crumpled blanket remains strewed over the couch from where I left it moments ago. With trembling fingers, I fold it before laying it over the back of the sofa.

In a voice so quiet, I barely recognize it as my own, I ask the question I don't want to hear the answer to, "It's Trevor, isn't it?"

"I'm Officer Wade and this is my partner, Officer Finch." He points to the petite blonde beside him. "Please, let's have a seat." His tone is even as he invites me to have a seat in my own home.

His face is a mask of professionalism, but for a split second, it hides nothing, and cold dread seeps into my pores.

"No. Please, I'd rather stand." A million horrific scenarios run through my head, each one worse than the last. This moment will be burned into my brain with such clarity years from now. I'll remember where I stood and exactly what I wore. In the next few seconds, my heart will shatter.

"Mrs. Salinger, it really would be best for you to take a seat," Officer Wade insists.

Their pitying eyes seem to assess each small step I take toward the chair. They settle on the couch, grim smiles replacing the pleasantries.

"Mrs. Salinger, I'm sorry to inform you that your husband, Trevor, has been involved in an accident," Officer Wade tells me.

My heart squeezes in my chest, and words wobble past my lips. "What do you mean, he's been involved in an accident?" My eyes flit to the clock on the wall. It's after two in the morning, and Trevor should've been home a few hours ago.

Oh God. Please. Please.

"A suspect fleeing a crime struck Mr. Salinger's vehicle," Officer Wade explains. "I'm so sorry, Mrs. Salinger. Your husband died on impact."

I shake my head in denial. "No! No." *He was on his way home to me.* "It's not him," I say defiantly. "There's been some sort of mistake." My arms wrap tightly around my middle, and tears sting my eyes. *Please let it be a mistake. This can't be happening.*

They look at me with sympathy in their eyes.

"Is there someone we can call for you?" Officer Finch asks.

Her words jumble in my head as the room begins to sway and spin.

"No. No. Please just go." When they make no attempt to leave, I repeat, "Please."

"Once again, we're so sorry for your loss, Mrs. Salinger. We'll show ourselves out," Officer Finch says.

I don't acknowledge them as they walk out the door. Or turn my head when the clicking of the doorknob echoes through our condo.

"Your husband died on impact."

Those five words warble and whir like scratched vinyl on a record player. I sink to the floor, my hands covering my ears to block out the sound.

"Your husband died on impact."

They strike with the strength of an F5 tornado, crushing bones and shattering my heart.

Vomit burns at the base of my esophagus. I struggle to get to my feet and clamp a hand over my mouth. Then, I hurry into the kitchen to heave the contents of my stomach into the trash can. I stagger to the cabinet for a glass and fill it beneath the water dispenser in the refrigerator door. My hand quakes so badly, the water sloshes from side to side, and I have to use both hands to steady it as I move to the sink. I lift the tumbler to my lips and swish the cold liquid in my mouth. Then, I lean over and spit down the drain. With the glass still clutched in my hand, I fall to my knees on the hardwood floor.

"Trevor!" I scream into the emptiness.

I hurl the glass at the wall. It splinters into a thousand tiny shards, much like my soul. I tuck my body into a fetal position, and my entire being shudders with the force of my sobs. The endless stream of tears distorts my vision. I roll to my side and press my cheek against the floor.

"Pl-please, G-god. Not Trev-or," I beg.

It hurts so much. I can't breathe.

I cry until everything around me fades to black.

Hours later, I wake up in bed with no memory of how I got here. I roll over and glide a hand across Trevor's pillowcase, the fabric is cold against my warm palm. For a split second, I wonder if he's in the kitchen, making coffee. Then, the memory of last night comes crashing over me in a tsunami of ruin. My hand finds its way to my mouth, repressing the sob.

Trevor. Oh God. Trevor.

I tuck my knees to my chest, and the tears start all over again.

A soft knock sounds from the other side of the bedroom door.

"Tessa? It's Dante. I'm coming in." It's the only warning I get before Trevor's half-brother walks into the room.

Pressing my hand harder against my lips, I shake my head. I'm trying so hard to keep the sobs in. Overwhelming loss, jagged and painful, overtakes me. The force of the silent cries rack my body. My hand slips, and silence is no more. The sounds piercing the air are otherworldly. It hurts. It hurts so fucking much.

"Tessa?"

The bed dips.

"Tessa! Come on, Tessa." Dante's eyes are wild, panicked.

It looks as though he's trying to say something, but the screaming is so loud that I can't hear him. His strong hands grip my arms and lift me from the mattress. He wraps me in a snug embrace and cradles me into him, burying my face against the crook of his neck. And I cry with a brokenness so guttural, the strength of it shakes our bodies as well as the bed. The harder I weep, the tighter Dante holds on to me.

Minutes, maybe hours, pass when I finally lift my head.

"Hey," he says, meeting my swollen eyes. His dark hair is disheveled. The skin below his eyes is darkened with shadows. Chocolate irises reveal sadness and shock. "Tessa...I'm so sorry."

My head pounds from crying. "I wa-want to wa-wake up." My breath is ragged and thick. "I wa-want th-this not to be real."

Dante's eyes are flecked with pain as my gaze locks on his. "I know, Tess. Me, too." He studies me for a minute, and

I know he has something more to say. "I came over last night as soon as I heard..." His voice trails off, and I realize how I got to bed.

Suddenly, sitting on his lap is awkward. I slide off and sit beside him, dropping my head into my hands.

"I went out earlier to pick up breakfast and coffee. I'll give you a few minutes." Dante stands and walks toward the door. His footsteps stop short.

I draw in a stuttered breath and wipe my eyes. "I-I'll b-be down in a few," I say, rising to my feet.

He turns back and crosses the carpet between us. When we're inches apart, he opens his arms and tugs me into his chest. I try to swallow past the lump in my throat as my arms encircle his waist. He securely holds me against him, wordlessly stroking my hair, and I can't stop the tears.

When he finally speaks, he says, "We'll get through this, Tessa, I promise." I sniffle, and he holds me closer and whispers, "I've got you. You don't have to do this on your own."

I don't see how I'm supposed to *get through this*. To keep breathing when the very foundation of my entire world has dropped from beneath me.

Without responding, I let his words hang in the air and step out of his embrace. There is a softness in Dante's normally intense stare. He walks away, and I gather my clothes before heading into the en suite bathroom. After I turn on the shower, I strip out of my pajamas.

The bathroom mirror fogs from the rising heat, and my reflection in the glass vanishes. There one minute and then...*gone.*

Just like Trevor.

I step beneath the water. The nearly too-hot spray stings, but I don't adjust the temperature. I'm driven by the need to feel something besides overwhelming grief. The torrent camouflages the tears streaming down my cheeks. I move through the motions on autopilot—my hair first and then my body. The bottle of Trevor's shower gel draws my attention. I reach for it, open the top, and squeeze it into my hand, inhaling his spicy sandalwood scent.

And it hits me. He'll never hold me in his arms again. We won't stroll through the city streets, hand in hand, or dance in Grant Park during Lollapalooza. There will be no more birthdays or holidays or ordinary days.

The heaviness of grief takes on a presence of its own. Loud sobs wrench from my throat, and I cover my mouth to suppress the sound. No longer able to stand under the weight of my despair, I fall to my knees and weep until the water runs cold.

In the blink of an eye, my whole world changed. And, for the life of me, I can't remember how to draw air into my lungs.

75902132R00183

Made in the USA
Columbia, SC
23 September 2019